KILL THE ALIENS!

The door was hurled wide and the men charged through it.

The lights were dim and at first they could see no one. They spread out, guns ready. An Oinn who had been concealed by a bank of instruments suddenly appeared. Rob was swinging up his gun when there was the rapid slapping sound of muffled firing from behind him and the alien went over and down.

They ran on. Another Oinn appeared, screeching something – but as the first sound emerged he spun about and fell, torn and bleeding from a dozen wounds. Then the soldiers spread out and searched the large chamber, the muzzles of their guns sniffing the air like hungry dogs.

'Empty,' Groot reported. 'Just the two of them here.'

'That means there are five more of them,' Rob said. 'Move it out. Search through their quarters. I want the five of them dead.'

Also by Harry Harrison in Sphere Books:

DEATHWORLD TRILOGY
PLAGUE FROM SPACE
THE STAINLESS STEEL RAT
THE STAINLESS STEEL RAT WANTS YOU
THE STAINLESS STEEL RAT'S REVENGE
THE STAINLESS STEEL RAT SAVES THE WORLD
THE STAINLESS STEEL RAT FOR PRESIDENT
PLANET OF NO RETURN

Invasion Earth

HARRY HARRISON

SPHERE BOOKS LIMITED
30–32 Gray's Inn Road, London WC1X 8JL

First published in Great Britain by
Sphere Books Ltd 1984
Copyright © 1982 by Harry Harrison

Published in the United States of America by
Ace Books, 1982

TRADE
MARK

Set in 10/11½ Compugraphic Mallard

Printed and bound in Great Britain by
Cox & Wyman Ltd, Reading

Contents

The Arrival

It came out of the Pacific Ocean just before dawn, bursting up over the horizon and screaming across the California coastline with meteoric speed. It was so fast that it was over Arizona before the first crash of its supersonic flight struck the ground. The explosion of sound blew out windows, activated countless burglar alarms, set every dog in its track to howling. At the same instant the military Early Warning radar exploded into life. Enemy attack!

The jet fighters were scrambled, ground to air missiles zeroed in, ICBMs readied in their silos. The whistle almost blew to start the big one–but not quite. There was just nothing orthodox about the trace that resembled an attacking missile. It came from the wrong place, at the wrong speed and the wrong altitude. It hurtled along at close to Mach-5 and it should have burnt up. It did not. When it changed speed, over Kansas, it did so abruptly, dropping to Mach-3. In less than thirty minutes it had crossed half of the United States, with aimed missiles tracking it all the way. They were not fired.

'*Nothing* is right about that thing,' a military radar controller said, speaking for all of them. 'We don't have a bird that can fly like that–and neither do the Russkies.'

'We hope,' his commanding officer said grimly, looking at the red telephone before him, waiting for an answer to his emergency call. The President would be on the Hot Line to Moscow right now, getting an answer to that very important question. He had the phone pressed to his ear the instant it began to ring. Listening closely, nodding. 'Yes, sir,' he said, hanging

1

the instrument up slowly. 'You're right. It's not the Russkies. They are as surprised as we are. Intelligence reports confirm that it couldn't possibly be theirs. But if not theirs . . .?'

It is significant that he did not speak aloud his thoughts about the possible origin of a craft like this one–nor did anyone else. They watched, dumbstruck, and waited.

Not for long. With an altitude change just as disconcerting and sudden as its earlier alteration in speed, it dropped to a thousand feet as it crossed the New Jersey Highlands and hurtled out over the Outer Bay. Then turned north towards Manhattan Island.

It did not do this in an arc. It simply turned a corner, changing its course by ninety degrees in a fractional instant of time. On the radar screens the course plot was an unbelievable L shape.

It was aiming towards the World Trade Center. The highest building in the world.

Sharon Forkner was standing and looking south out of a window on the ninetieth floor at that very moment, staring unseeingly at the magnificent view, thinking about what she had to get at the deli on the way home. A glint of light on the horizon drew her attention. She glanced at it, at the black speck growing beneath it, growing and swelling in a frantic heartbeat of time. Something immense and dark hurtling directly at her– then past with an explosion of sound. A foot high gouge was ripped through the fabric of the building not ten feet from her as some portion of the thing brushed against the Trade Tower. Particles of plaster and a cloud of dust boiled out, then cleared to reveal the long gap in the wall with sunlight pouring in. She fainted, falling limply against the desk then sliding slowly to the floor.

As though the Trade Towers had been its target, the vehicle began dropping as soon as it had passed between them. Its speed slowed from supersonic to subsonic before it had crossed Forty-second Street. It was scant feet above the midtown skyscrapers and

2

falling like a rock as it came over Fifty-ninth Street. Its dark form blotted out the sun; people looked up, horrified, as it dropped towards them. Just clearing the Central Park Zoo to crash headlong into the grassy slope beyond. Plowing a rut in the ground before coming to a stop. A park attendant was obliterated by its landing, as was a nurse pushing an expensive baby carriage. They were the only casualties.

In the silence that followed its arrival screams and shouts could now be heard, and the shrill blast of a police whistle. The first sirens sounded in the distance.

1. Intruder from the Sky

New York is a city that knows how to move fast. Within five minutes a police cordon had pushed the bystanders back a hundred yards from the grounded object. Two photographers were snapping pictures over the cops' shoulders while a cine buff was dragged out of a tree, still grinding away happily. Almost as the thing touched the ground the switchboard at the *Daily News* lit up–cash awards are given to people who phone in news tips–while the fire trucks arrived at the same time as the squad cars. When the military helicopter landed a good thirty-five minutes later, the situation was well in hand.

'I'll take command of the situation now,' the general said, swinging down from his helicopter.

'You're under arrest,' the grizzled police captain said, his face registering all the emotion of a chunk of granite. He pointed a finger like a loaded gun at the helicopter pilot. 'You have ten seconds to lift that thing off and out of this area. Move.'

'You can't . . .!' the general shouted just as two policemen did, pulling his arms behind his back and clamping cuffs about his wrists. The copter pilot took one look at this and kicked the engine into life. The roar of the blades drowned out the general's voice which was all for the best.

Rob Hayward had reached the police cordon just in time to witness the incident. He permitted himself one grin of intense satisfaction before wiping all emotion from his face. Taking out his wallet with his identification he moved forward through the line.

'I am Colonel Robert Hayward, Air Force Intelligence. This is my identification.'

The police captain looked at the man who had appeared at his side. Tall, solid, blue eyes in a tanned face, a nose broken more than once. The captain glanced at the ID.

'What do you want, colonel?' he asked.

'To supply you with some information. That object out there crossed the West Coast about an hour ago. We tracked it here. We have no idea what it is. An official investigation team and Army personnel are on their way now to relieve you. With Presidential authorization. Until they arrive I respectfully suggest that you move your cordon back at least another hundred yards and begin to clear the streets and buildings in the immediate area.'

The captain nodded. 'I appreciate those suggestions, colonel, and will put them into effect.' He had to raise his voice to be heard over the hoarse bellowing of the handcuffed officer. Rob Hayward leaned close as he spoke again.

'Your prisoner is General Hawker, commander of the Governor's Island garrison. Do you think you could release him in my custody? Outside your police lines of course.'

'I know who the son of a bitch is. You can have him if you want him.' A thin smile vanished as soon as it appeared on that leathery face. 'I just wanted to make a jurisdictional point.'

It was dark by the time the military units had replaced the police, but the banks of searchlights turned the park as bright as day. There had been no changes. The scarred, ninety-foot-long wedge of blue metal lay dormant and mute. Guns of every calibre were trained on the thing, as well as the massed banks of recording instruments. Rob Hayward stood with the small group of officers and scientists who were deciding on the next step.

'We can get a volunteer to go hammer on the thing,' an armored cavalry general said.

'We *had* been thinking of some form of communication a little more sophisticated,' one of the scientific

6

team sniffed. 'Radio broadcasts, changing frequencies, infrared and ultraviolet . . .'

'A thirty inch round from a naval gun would let them know we're here,' an admiral said.

Rob Hayward kept his peace. Chance had put him on the spot; as East Coast director of Air Force Intelligence he didn't visit New York that often, and he intended to make the most of it. His recording teams were already in position. The brass could make the opening moves; he would follow up when events entered his jurisdiction. For the moment he was just going to observe . . .

The loudspeaker on the communications trailer rustled into life and the voice of one of the operators boomed out.

'We're receiving short wave radiation from the thing. And sounds of some kind . . .'

His voice was drowned out by metallic creaking from the object before them–followed by an explosive bang as a great slab of metal dropped from the craft's side. The gunners crouched over their sights, fingers poised on the triggers.

'Hold your fire!' an imperious voice cracked out. 'Unless there is an order there will be no firing.'

The man who had spoken, General Beltine, stepped forward and turned to face the ranked troops. An old-fashioned swagger stick slapped against his thigh as he glowered at the soldiers; their fingers relaxed. Only when he was sure that his command had been understood did he turn about and face the silent opening with the others.

Nothing more happened. After one minute the general signalled one of his aides and gave a command. The man hurried to the waiting officers, scanning their faces as they looked eagerly at him. He came up to Rob Hayward and saluted.

'General wishes to see you, colonel.' Rob returned the salute and followed him forward.

'Orders from the Pentagon,' Beltine said. 'If that thing shows no signs of aggression that have to be immediately countered then I am to put Plan L67 into action. That's you and your team, right?'

'Yes, general. L67 is one of the contingency plans drawn up for use in case of an emergency of this kind.'

'Don't tell me you were expecting *this* to happen?'

'We weren't expecting anything to happen, sir. We just have plans for a number of situations of emergency. May I proceed?'

'Is your team here?'

'Yes, sir.'

'Then–go ahead. And good luck.'

Rob spoke quietly into his two-way, then turned back towards the lines of troops and vehicles. L67. One of the blue-sky plans that everyone had laughed at. What if a flying saucer lands? What then? Ha-ha. Not only weren't they laughing now–they probably weren't even smiling.

He pulled open the flap of the tent and stepped in. Sergeant Groot held out the web belt with Rob's equipment already attached. The sergeant was six foot six, big and black and just as mean as he looked. He had left South Africa when he was still a teenager–the police there were still looking for him–and had immediately enlisted in the US Army upon arrival here. His combat record was an astonishing one, as was his reputation as an unarmed defense expert. He had been working with Rob for over six years and their relation was one of mutual respect.

'What do we know about that thing?' Groot asked.

'Absolutely nothing. There is an open door. We go in blind. Are you ready, Shetly?'

Corporal Shetly nodded in response, adjusting the clips on the heavy communication pack on his back. He was gangly and thin, with a protruding Adam's apple; he looked and sounded like a dim ridge-runner from the Tennessee mountains. He was also an electronics specialist who could work and repair any device manufactured by man. He settled the reel into position on his hip and paid out a length of wire. 'Recordin' now,' he said, activating the TV camera with attendant pickups.

8

'Let's go then.' Rob tightened his helmet strap and switched on the light fixed into place on it. They went out smoothly, one, two, three, just as they had practiced a hundred times.

His backup squad was waiting. They fell into position to the rear without being given any commands. As they proceeded, soldier after soldier dropped behind to guard the thin communication wire that stretched back to the recorders in the tent. The signal was being radio broadcast as well, but the signal would undoubtedly cut out as soon as the pickups were inside the metal shell. The wire was their backup. The cordon of troops opened ranks as they approached, then closed in behind them. Rob led the way forward, stopping only when he was within arm's length of the vessel.

'The opening is in front of me,' he said, the microphones picking up and recording his words. 'Rectangular. About eight feet high. Metal wall a foot thick at least. Metal wall inside as well, floor, light blue, no patterns, no markings. The corridor turns. Nothing else visible. We're going in.'

He moved. Jumping over the low sill and landing with a clang on the floor inside, not slowing until he reached the turn in the corridor. He stopped there and waited for the others to catch up.

'Communications?' he asked.

'In the green on everythin', colonel. Making a damn fine home movie.'

'Stay close. If I need support I want it fast.' Groot's noncommittal grunt was the only answer, but he knew what it meant. He would get all the backup he needed when he needed it.

'Proceeding down the corridor.'

He led the way, one slow step at a time, stopping suddenly when Shetly spoke.

'Radio reception and broadcast gone. Everythin's goin' out on the wire now.'

'Doors ahead. I'm stopping at the first one. No handle. An orange-colored disc in the center. I'm going to touch the disc . . .'

Rob reached forward slowly, aware of Sergeant Groot's large form moving up close behind him. He never touched the door. When his fingers were still six inches away the mechanism was actuated. There was a sharp clicking sound and the door dropped out of sight into the sill.

As they looked in, Rob could not control a sudden gasped intake of breath. Behind him Shetly muttered an oath under his breath. Only Groot was silent, but the muzzle of his .45 automatic quested forward slowly until Rob pushed it aside.

'We won't need weapons,' he said hoarsely, then cleared his throat. 'For the record. The door is now open and we are looking into what appears to be the control room of this craft. There are banks of instruments of many kinds, plus viewing screens that show remarkably clear pictures of the surroundings. The pilots, if that is what they are, both appear to be dead. One is on the deck beside his chair. The other still seated, but slumped to one side. Both have what appear to be multiple wounds. The one on the floor is lying in what might be a pool of blood. I say "might" because the congealed liquid is . . . green. These creatures do not appear to be human in any way. I am going closer.'

Rob slowly entered the room, his team keeping pace behind him. Groot's gun nosing in all directions for any possible attackers. There were none. Just the two at the controls. Rob moved closer, then waved to Shetly who was hanging back.

'Get that camera closer, corporal.'

'Got a telescopic lens on now, colonel. I don't rightly favor gettin' too close . . .'

'I want that camera right beside me. Just turn your head aside if you're going to flip your cookies.'

'I just might!'

'Right there. Hold it. The subject appears to be about seven feet tall. It is wearing a harness of some kind with various instruments attached to it, but no other clothing. It is covered with matted dark fur however, so anatomical details are not clear. It has suffered numerous cuts and contusions. The skin on its . . . hands is dark, with six, no seven fingers. Spatulate. No nails, but there appear to be small claws on the tip of each finger. It has two eyes, no visible ears, slits for a nose covered with a leathery sort of flap. The mouth is hanging open. It has teeth like . . . a shark. Pointed and serrated, two rows of them. The thing is, well, *ugly*. That's the only word for it. Not something I would like to meet on a dark night!' Rob turned away, not realizing that he shuddered as he did. The creature was repulsive, would have been so even without the terrible oozing wounds.

'I'll come back to this room after we take a look at the rest of the vehicle.'

Rob led the way from the chamber and continued down the hall, his team behind him, commenting for the record as he went.

'In the corridor again. No markings or artifacts of any kind here, though there are five more doors opening off of it, identical with the first one. I am going to open them in order. Approaching the first of these now.'

Rob hesitated, not knowing why, perhaps not wanting to face what possibly lay behind the metal wall before him. He could feel the hairs on the back of his neck stir–this was stupid! Emotional. He slammed his hand forward.

The door snapped down and out of sight and the great, fur-covered form hurled itself forward. It was screeching in a high-pitched wail, eyes open and glaring.

The weapon in its hand swinging towards them.

2. Inside the Ship

A reflex of fear kicked Rob to one side. As he fell he saw a line of flame reach out from the creature's gun, heard a scream of pain. Then the earsplitting hammer of the .45 thundered close by his head as Groot pumped shot after shot into the attacker. The heavy slugs jerked it back, spun it aside, tore at his head; one bullet in each eye, then more into its body. The creature folded and slumped and Rob pulled himself to one side so that it wouldn't drop on him.

It hit face down–then shuddered once as there was a muffled explosion under its body. After that it lay still. In the silence that followed the clatter of the clip from the automatic sounded loudly as it hit the floor. There was a quick snik-klak as Groot slipped in a fresh clip.

'If you'll move aside, colonel, I'll turn the thing over. Make sure it's down. Ten slugs should have done for it.'

The gun was aimed and ready in his right hand as Groot turned the creature over with one mighty heave of his left hand. The sightless eyes stared back at him.

'Looks like the weapon exploded,' he said, pointing to the creature's mangled hand and the destroyed weapon.

Rob nodded. 'The thing's finished. Now let's check the room.'

The sergeant went in fast and low and was out again seconds later. 'Plenty of machinery, stuff like that. No lockers or anything big enough to hold one of those. Otherwise empty.'

Rob dismissed any danger from this flank, and as he did so he remembered the gasp of pain he had heard earlier. He turned towards Shetly and saw that he was down, his hand clamped over his bloodsoaked shoul-

12

der, but the camera still pointed and recording.

'Just pinked me, nothin' to worry bout,' Shetly said.

'Let me see it. Groot, keep us covered.'

Shetly winced when Rob opened the communication pack harness, then cut away his clothing. A neat hole. Whatever the weapon was it had punched a hole right through the corporal's body, just below his clavicle. Rob tried to remember his anatomy. Plenty of muscles, muscle attachments here, no major blood vessels. Though it might have gone through his shoulder blade. The blood was already clotting as he shook antibiotic powder into the entrance and exit wounds and put pressure bandages into place over them.

'Put your arm through your jacket, here, it will work like a sling. We'll get you back . . .'

'No way. I can work the camera one-handed. We started this thing, colonel. Now let's get it finished.'

Rob thought for a second, then nodded agreement. This team was integrated, knew how to work together. If Shetly could hack it the best thing they could do was finish the job.

'All right. We go on. But sing out the second you're in trouble. Got that?'

'Yes, sir.'

'Good.' He helped Shetly to his feet, then took out his own .45 and pumped a round into the chamber and snicked the safety off. 'We'll go through the rest of the ship now. But treat it like a combat recon. Stay aside when the doors open. Shoot at any movement. Ready, sergeant?'

Groot nodded slowly, never taking his gaze from the empty corridor before them, his weapon pointed and ready. Rob took the point and the others fell into position behind him. Walking slowly and carefully towards the next door. Shetly stayed back out of range, camera trained, as the others took position on each side of the entrance. Rob brought the muzzle of his gun close to the circular marking on the door–then jumped back as it snapped open. Nothing moved. Groot went through in a rush and Rob followed him. A massive machine filled most of the room. None of the creatures was hidden there.

'Three more doors,' Rob said when they were back in the corridor. 'We'll hit them the same way.'

Tension–then anticlimax. Nothing. Twice in a row. Then they were at the last door. Once again they took positions and the colonel extended his gun. Nothing happened, even after the muzzle touched the metal surface. 'Locked,' he said, pushing at the immobile metal. 'Why just this one?' He thought for a long moment, then touched the control on the side of his helmet. 'Can you read me, support? Good. You've watched all this? Right. I want a volunteer to bring in an oxyacetylene torch. Right now. What? Negative, sir. No way that can be done. We pull out when we're finished. One more door then it's all yours. Right. We'll hold right here until it arrives. Out.'

Shetly slumped down and sat against the metal wall while they waited. Groot stayed on his guard, but his forehead puckered with thought.

'Colonel–what are these hairy damn things?'

'I have no idea, sergeant. Other than that they don't come from Earth. Neither does this flying machine.'

'Things from Mars?'

'Not Mars or Venus–or anywhere else in our solar system. They're from outside, from the stars you could say. Once this ship is cleared we'll see if the technical teams will find out more about them.'

'I don't like it, no little bit of it,' Groot growled.

'I couldn't agree more . . .'

They both spun about at a sudden clatter behind them–then relaxed as a frightened soldier hurried up, moving as fast as he could under the weight of the torch.

'Drop that and get out,' Rob ordered.

'Yes, *sir!*' He had the torch unlatched and on the deck and had turned and left even as he spoke.

Rob picked up the torch, but Groot took it from him. 'You just stand back and cover me, colonel. I've done this before.'

The big sergeant took the shielded dark glasses from their pocket and slipped them on, then snapped his spark. The brilliant blue flame lanced out. He adjusted it to his satisfaction, then bent close to the metal door. Rob stood to one side, intent, gun ready.

After a moment the metal began to glow and melt. As soon as a hole had been punched through it near the frame the sergeant began to work the opening downwards. It went slowly, the metal was tough, but the cut gradually lengthened.

When the opening had extended halfway down the door, as far as the colored circle, it must have touched some interior mechanism. There was a flare of sparks and the door began to move. Groot hurled himself to one side, turning off the torch and tearing out his automatic pistol as he rolled. Rob was crouched on the other side, his weapon ready as well.

It was dark inside, the illumination of the hallway penetrating only a few feet past the door. Nothing moved. With his free hand, Rob slowly took off his helmet and placed it on the floor—then switched on the light mounted on top of it as he jumped aside.

The beam revealed dark shapes. Machinery. Containers of some kind. He reached out and moved the helmet with his toe. More of the same. Then in the other direction. Something white against the far wall.

'It moved!' Groot called out. 'It moved, whatever it is! Aim the light—I'm going in.'

The sergeant was through the door, unbelievably fast for a man his size, staying away from the beam of light as it swung about. It held on the figure they had seen and Groot had his gun aimed, his finger touching the trigger.

Two white arms raised—no, not raised, held there. Chained to the wall. The head turning towards him. Lips moving.

'Tovarich . . . pomagat. . .'

'A Russky!' Groot said, shaking his head in unbelief. 'He's speaking Russian!'

3. An Alien Encounter

Colonel Rob Hayward picked up his helmet and aimed it so that the light burned down onto the captive figure.

'Maybe he's speaking Russian,' Rob said. 'But he's certainly no kind of Russian that I have ever seen before. What did he say?'

'Tovarich. Pomagat. Friend, help. But I ain't no friend of *that!'*

Only at first glance, in the semi-darkness, had the creature appeared even slightly human. Now, in the harsh light, they could see that its white covering was hairless and unwrinkled, looking more like hard plastic than normal skin. The oval head sat directly on the shoulders without a trace of any neck. Two large eyes, as multi-faceted as those of an insect, stared up at them. The mouth was a straight slice across the lower face. On each side of the skull were a scattering of irregular openings, one of which was opening and closing regularly. Only the creature's arms resembled human arms, originated in the region of the shoulders, though there appeared to be one joint too many in them. The arms terminated in two large digits, arranged like opposed thumbs. Metal rings were sealed about the arms, just below these strangely shaped hands, and fastened with chains to stretch the arms above the head to a fixture high on the wall. One of the openings in the side of the creature's head gaped slowly open and it began to speak slowly. Its mouth remained closed.

'Is it this . . . other language that you are speaking?'

The words were understandable enough, though spoken in a thick accent and overlayed with a harsh buzzing sound.

'Yes, we speak English,' Rob said, then threw a glance over his shoulder at Corporal Shetly. 'Are you getting all this?'

'Loud and clear, colonel. Though that don't mean I gotta believe it.'

'I am . . . painful,' the creature buzzed. 'It is my arms that are painful.'

'What is your name?' Rob asked, ignoring the thing's request. Its position looked very satisfactory to him for the moment.

'I am called Hes'bu. I am of the Oinn. I am painful.'

'I'm going to take care of that pain in just one minute, Hes'bu. You just answer a few questions first and then everything will be fine. Do you know anything about the very large and ugly creatures that were operating this vehicle . . .?'

His words had a distinct effect on the captive. Its eyes dulled and the thin white arms shivered in their manacles. *'Blettr . . .'* The words were hissed loudly and at the same instant the mouth opened for the first time in some unrecognizable expression. It was sharp-edged, like a parrot's beak, and dark inside. The shiver passed through its form again and its eyes sparkled again in the light. 'Hurting,' it said.

Rob made a sudden decision. Hes'bu would have to be released from the chains sooner or later. Sooner might prejudice it more favorably in their direction. Cooperation would help because there were a lot of questions that needed to be asked.

'We'll get you out of the chains,' he said. 'Is there a release?'

'There, high above me at the top of the room. A colored plate to be touched.'

It was a smaller version of the actuators on the doors. Groot reached up and put his hand near it. Something clicked in the wall and the manacles dropped free. He stepped back, gun ready.

Hes'bu's arms dropped heavily and the creature slumped forward, head lowered. But only for a moment. Then it stood up, rising in a single lithe

17

movement. When it did Rob saw that both its legs were made of jointed, shiny metal. Everything about this creature was alien; there were so many questions he wanted to ask that he had no idea where to begin. He switched on his communication connection.

'Has the decon trailer arrived yet? Good. Let me know when it's sealed over the door to this ship. Meanwhile I'll get what intelligence I can.' He broke the connection and turned to Hes'bu. 'I have a number of questions to ask you.'

'Do not ask them. I have no answers for you.'

'I am painful . . .'

Rob spoke the words in a reasonable imitation of Hes'bu's accent. He had done it on sudden impulse–but did not regret it. They had helped the prisoner, perhaps saved its life, and all they asked in return were answers to some very important questions. And his imitation of the other's voice was a test as well. Was it intelligent enough to understand the meaning behind his mockery? A small reminder that they had come to Hes'bu's rescue.

The alien looked steadily at Rob for a long, silent moment, then lowered its head. 'You do well to make me remember my pain and your helping me. I am grateful. But there is too much you don't understand. I have difficulty. I have . . . is *oath* the right word? Yes? Oath not to reveal. Difficulty. Question. The Blettr. Do they live?'

'No. The two at the controls were dead. A third attacked us and was killed. Are there any more?'

'No. Only the three. Now I must order my thinking. After which I will tell you what you need to know.'

Rob's superiors had been following this exchange closely and his earphones scratched to life a moment later. His instructions were clear.

'I have been ordered to take you from this ship to a decontamination vehicle waiting outside. There are communications facilities there for the team that will interrogate you.'

'Some of your words, they are not easy to understand.'

Rob smiled coldly. 'I'm the contact man. My job is

18

finished when I get you safely out of here. Experts will take over from me then and talk to you.'

Hes'bu nodded, but said nothing. Rob led the way into the corridor and the others followed. Sergeant Groot's hand was near his gun at all times; he trusted no one–or no thing.

Hes'bu glanced down at the dead Blettr when they passed the corpse, but said nothing. He glanced in silence into the control room as well. An airlock had been sealed over the exit from the ship and they passed through it into the decontamination trailer beyond. While they closed and sealed the door, Hes'bu crossed to the nearest window and looked out. There was the quick flare of flashguns from the military photographers waiting outside. The strong flashes must have hurt for he turned away quickly, his arm before his eyes, and surveyed the inside of the trailer.

'What is this?' Hes'bu asked, pointing to the TV cameras that Shetly was setting up, and the row of TV screens behind them.

'You will sit there and face the camera,' Rob explained. 'The interview team will appear on the screens and ask you questions.'

'They will not be here themselves, in real?'

'In the flesh? No. This is going to be done by remote.'

Hes'bu turned about and his metal feet clacked on the floor as he walked to the far end of the trailer. Out of sight of the cameras. 'You will tell them no,' he said. 'I will talk to you and no one else.'

Rob signalled to Corporal Shetly. 'Fire up the portable again,' he ordered, then turned back. 'The authorities won't like this decision. They are going to ask why.'

'An answer is simple. There is the same word in your language as mine. Honor. You came in person to the ship and found me and fought and killed the Blettr. You came in flesh. That is honor.' He waved in the direction of the TV setup. 'Pictures by electricity have no honor. I talk to you.'

The telephone rang and Rob went reluctantly to answer it. General Beltine surprised him.

'I have just spoken to the President. He has watched everything that happened from the time you entered that ship. He wishes to congratulate you on the way you have handled the situation. He also asked me to inform you that he has overruled his advisors in this matter and wishes you to continue the interrogation of the alien. He feels that we don't need experts to ask the questions that are begging for answers. Go to it, colonel.'

'Thank you, sir. I'll do my best.'

This was it. His responsibility. It had almost been easier to walk into the ship and face the unknown. They would all be looking over his shoulders now, from the President right on down through the Pentagon and everyone else. Any mistakes he made would be instantly seen. The hell with it! All he could do was ask the questions, do his best. They could follow up afterwards if they wanted to know any more. The general was right—the obvious questions were screaming for answers.

'All right, Hes'bu,' he said. 'I'm the one who will be interrogating you.' The alien nodded agreement. 'First and more important. Who are the Blettr, the creatures that were operating this ship?'

'They are a species of creatures who hate all other intelligent life forms. They are like an insane disease. They moved out of their home star system some–thousands of thousands of years ago in your time scale–and have been killing ever since.'

'And your race, the Oinn, what is your relationship to them?'

'We try to survive. No more. We fight and we retreat.'

'Will you explain your presence aboard the crashed ship?'

'There was a battle, a large one, during which my own ship was destroyed. I was unconscious or they would never have captured me.'

'Do you know why they came here? Landed on Earth?'

'I can only guess since I talked to none of them. I looked at the bodies in the control room. Their ship was obviously hit by–I know no words in your language. It is a weapon of ours that changes things when it hits in a different way. They were wounded, dying, their ship out of control . . . yes!' Hes'bu sprang to his feet. 'I looked outside. There are large buildings. Is there a major city nearby?'

'We are in the center of New York City. One of the largest and most important on Earth . . .'

'I must re go into the ship!' The alien was across the room as he spoke, clumsily working the sealing controls on the door. Groot had his automatic out and aimed, but Rob waved him back.

'What's wrong?' he asked.

'Inside!'

The door opened and Hes'bu plunged through–with Rob right behind him, the others following after. Hes'bu ran down the corridor and into the control room where he stopped to examine the banks of instruments. He apparently found what he wanted because he hurried to a panel and was reaching up to it when Rob called out loudly.

'Stop! Do you see this weapon in my hand? It is the same as the one that killed the Blettr in the corridor. It can kill you. If you touch anything on that board I will fire. Now lower your hands.'

Hes'bu did so, slowly, turning about.

'Do not stop me. I must . . .'

'Do what–and why?'

'Make this not to work. Turn off the control, here, on the main thrust control, see, it must be stopped. That was why they landed here.'

'Why?'

'In dying to destroy. Knowing they were to dying. Make of this ship a great bomb to destroy this city and in all directions. Now, please, there is no time left. I must make it not to work!'

4. Intelligence Report

'Don't touch anything! I will fire if you do!' Rob snapped on his communicator. 'Patch me to General Beltine, emergency. General? You heard? Do you have instructions, sir? Yes, sir, I'll wait.'

They stood in silence then, all four of them, three human and one alien, waiting. Rob and the sergeant had their guns trained and ready. Corporal Shetly took one step backward, then stopped. There was no walking away from this one. The silence stretched on and on . . .

'Right!' Rob said in answer to an unheard command. He lowered his gun. 'They said go ahead. They have no option but to believe you.'

Hes'bu had turned about at the first words, his paired, spatulate fingers prodding at the board. He made three rapid movements and stepped back. There was a sudden clicking sound–loud in the frozen silence. Then all of the lights on the board went out.

'It is done.' Hes'bu slumped visibly. 'We return to the question chamber.'

Hes'bu asked for water and was given a glass. That's one question answered at least, Rob thought. They breathe our air and drink water, so they must have carbon-based metabolisms like ours. He drank some water himself but wished that it had been heavily laced with scotch. Later. This job had to be done first. He thought about the next question and decided to approach it indirectly.

'When we first saw you, you spoke to us in Russian. Then you changed to English. How do you know these languages?'

'Radio. Your broadcasts are very strong. Experts

22

intercept and prepare lessons in the two languages most heard. We learn them. Interesting to do.'

Interesting!, Rob thought. What sort of brains did the Oinn have to enable them to learn this many languages with such little effort? Yet what was the reason for this? He spoke the question aloud.

'Why listen to our broadcasts–and learn our languages?'

'Because we have been afraid for a long time, many of your centuries, that this planet will be next. In our defensive battle against the Blettr we retreat and we are followed. We are being pushed further and further from our home worlds, making our battle that much more difficult. In this retreat we have unknowingly led the enemy to your planet. We have honor. We feel guilt about what we have done, even though it was not on purpose done. Therefore we learn your languages and prepare for the day when you must be told. We did not plan it to happen like this, but that day has now come.'

Rob's eyes narrowed in thought; he did not like this. 'Are you trying to tell me that there is some kind of war going on? And that you want to enlist this planet to battle on your side of the galactic conflict? Are you trying to lead us into war?'

'No, not that all. We must now tell you that you will be attacked. We will help you all that we can to defend yourselves.'

'That is very generous of you–considering that you led the attackers here.'

'Not on purpose done!'

'Of course. But still done. What if we decide not to get involved in this conflict?'

'It is not a matter of decision with Blettr. They discover you, they destroy you. All living intelligence their enemies. From space the bombs of destruction. We can supply weapons of planetary defense if you permit us.'

Rob sighed and stretched; he suddenly realized how exhausted he had become. 'Happily for me,' he said, 'that is not my decision to make. I simply ask the questions. It will be up to the authorities to decide what

23

actions should be taken. I'll be back in a moment.'

Rob went to the service area and found the medical kit. He took out the jar of amphetamines and swallowed two of them. This was going to be a long session.

It went on for five long hours more before Hes'bu suddenly announced that he would answer no more questions because of fatigue. They all needed the rest, all except Sergeant Groot.

'Get some sleep, sir,' he said. 'I'll just sit here a bit and keep an eye on our friend. You too, Shetly, just set up the recorder to keep running by itself.'

'Are you sure?' Rob said.

'No sweat, colonel. Got a lot to think about.'

'Don't we all.'

'That's the truth. And I've been thinking of a question or two myself. Like why this turkey has got steel legs.'

'A good question, and I intend to ask it. Make a memo of any more ideas you have like this. I imagine the general and the staff will have some of their own as well. I'm going to get some rack–but wake me up as soon as Hes'bu stirs.'

Only moments seemed to have passed before Rob felt the firm hand steadily shaking his shoulder. He blinked his eyes open to see Groot standing there, holding out a cup of black coffee.

'Is Hes'bu awake?' he asked, smacking his dry lips together.

'No, sir. It's just been about two hours. But General Beltine is on the phone.'

'All right. I'll be right there.' Rob sat up, yawning, then sipped a mouthful of coffee before he stumbled over to the phone. 'General?'

'*It looks like there's another emergency coming together, Rob. I can't tell you in person because the medics still haven't given the ship or our visitor a clean bill of health. So I'm sending someone in to brief you. Along with a doctor for your wounded man.*'

'Yes, sir.' There was little else that he could say. What kind of an emergency could possible involve him?

24

He couldn't think–but knew that he had better be able to soon. Two more of the bennies, washed down with the coffee. They gave him a stabbing heartburn, but at least brought him to life. There was a sudden rattling as the sealed door was unlocked. Rob went to wash some of the sleep out of his eyes and when he came back he could only blink dazedly at the girl standing next to the great bulk of Sergeant Groot.

Black eyes, long black hair, a heart-shaped face, full but graceful figure . . .

'Nadia Andrianova,' he said. She nodded.

'And you are Colonel Robert Hayward. We meet for the first time.'

She stepped forward and shook his hand, firmly, one time up and down in the French manner. Although they had never met before, they each knew a good deal about the other. Rob had seen her once, at a distance, at an embassy reception. An associate from the CIA had pointed her out to him.

'Lovely, isn't she? Skin like peaches and cream. Mind like a steel beaver trap. Started out as a translator for OGPU. Kept adding languages–must speak at least fifteen by now. Moved on to analyst and now she is head of the US section of intelligence in Washington. Wish we had her on our team.'

'A field agent?' Rob had asked.

'No. Nothing like that. More valuable than a dozen goons–and strictly legal. Reads everything printed in this country, from weather charts to local newspapers, and puts it all together. A very bright lady.'

And now she was here. In the center of what Rob had thought was a classified security operation. All very confusing, particularly when you still aren't awake.

'Please, sit down,' Rob said. 'Would you like some coffee?' Wonderful, he thought, playing mine host; but it was all he could think to say.

'Thank you, no. But I would like some tea. Black, strong, just sugar.'

'I'll take care of that,' Groot said.

'Do you know what's happening outside?' Nadia

asked, placing her large shoulder bag on the floor beside the chair then sitting down across from Rob, then crossing her legs. Very nice, he thought, blinking at them then burying his face in his coffee.

'What do you mean?' he asked, swallowing.

'Your interview with the alien. Do you know that it was transmitted live to the United Nations?'

'They forgot to tell me. I assumed this was all top security.'

'Hardly,' she said, flaring her nostrils slightly in disdain at the thought. 'Your country and mine have been in constant communication since the alien craft entered your airspace. Some attempt was made by your military authorities to keep events secret, but your President wisely overruled them.'

Rob had a good idea of the amount of infighting that lay behind her words. The hawks in the department wanting to sit on the whole thing. A liberal President who believed in open government. The press blanketing the world with coverage. The other countries pushing for information. Nadia nodded, as though following his thoughts.

'Reports have been given to the press, without all the details of course. But the UN ambassadors have watched everything. It is due to this unusual cooperation that my nation has been able to make a valuable contribution. You know of course of our science satellite, *Pitnatset?*'

Rob nodded. 'Radio star research, in geostationary orbit over the Black Sea.'

'All current research projects were cancelled when the alien ship appeared. It has been utilized as a highly sensitive search radar and receiver since then. No unidentified objects have yet been discovered in nearby space, but of course the search is a slow and careful one and will take a good deal of time.'

'But you have come up with something–or you wouldn't be here.'

'That is correct. A number of radio broadcasts have been received and recorded. They appear to emanate

26

roughly from the direction of Jupiter. Some are quite clear and they have been analyzed. I have aided in this. It was of my opinion, since verified by the Department of Languages in Moscow University, that the language being spoken is not of human origin.'

'Then the next step is obvious,' Rob stood and stretched. 'We see if our friend inside can do a translation for us. Do you have copies?

Nadia dug into her large bag and produced a small recorder. She placed it on the table and slipped a micro cassette into it, then pressed the *play* button. There was a whistle of static, then a rumbling voice spoke.

'*N'slht nweu bnnju kloi ksjhhsbn bsu . . .*'

Rob shook his head with incomprehension and Nadia turned it off. 'Certainly nothing that I ever heard of. Unless it is spoken code . . .'

'Do not turn it off, play more,' Hes'bu said, appearing in the doorway to the other room.

'Do you know what this broadcast is?' Nadia asked. She did not seem at all bothered by the alien's presence.

'It is my language. A ship to ship transmission. I did not know we had ships in this solar system. Perhaps they followed the Blettr ship. Please, I must hear more.'

Rob looked over at the freshly bandaged Corporal Shetly who was yawning widely while he set up his recording apparatus. 'Are you getting this?' Rob asked.

'On the tape and on the wire, sir.'

'Good.' Rob turned back to Hes'bu. 'We are going to play the tape now, but only if you give a running translation of it. Is that agreed?'

'Yes, of course. Now the playing.'

Most of what was said was incomprehensible, even though the alien labored to translate it. Ship to ship communication is technical shorthand discussing orbits, passing on commands, a few bits of what appeared to be personal chat. Then Hes'bu hesitated, became excited.

'Something important coming. An overcall . . . over-

27

ride announcement. These are only for matters of great urgency.'

The crosstalk ceased and there was a short silence before a single voice broke in, talking fast, rattling out the phrases. Hes'bu was silent, leaning forward and listening intently. He made no attempt to translate. Rob waited a few moments longer–then leaned over and turned off the machine.

'No, don't!' Hes'bu wailed. 'Continue the playing!'

'You're not translating.'

'I know, yes, no–a moment longer, I am begging, then the complete translation. Message not complete.'

Rob hesitated, then reached to turn it back on. 'We want that translation.'

Hes'bu stared into space as the words crackled out, and his mouth dropped slowly open. Then he signalled with his paired fingers, a clicking motion like scissors blades, and his mouth clacked shut.

'Message finished,' he said. 'You must contact your authorities at once, all authorities of different languages all over your world. It is for them to hear . . .'

'What was the message,' Rob broke in. 'Tell us now. The authorities are listening.'

'Coming soon. Those were scout ships of my people who are watching an attacking fleet of the Blettr. Their course is certain. They come here, to Earth. The war now comes to your planet. You cannot stop it. I am most regretful.'

Hes'bu hesitated, his fingers clicking together nervously, then he spoke. 'The scouts are sure that a large attack vessel is in this fleet. If that is true that is very, very bad news for your planet. Very bad indeed.'

5. The Quest

The door of the trailer burst open and a shaft of bright sunlight lanced into the darkened interior. General Beltine stood in the opening, flexing his swagger stick in both hands.

'The medics have called an end to the quarantine,' he announced. 'Dissected the bodies from the ship. Anything those might have we can't catch. Metabolism is too alien. So we're moving the interrogation to the Pentagon.' He pointed the stick at Nadia as she started to speak. 'Don't worry, young lady, this is a combined operation. Your team is there already. The news media don't have the whole story yet, but it's sure to leak from that crowd at the UN. We want you, Colonel Hayward, and Hes'bu in Washington before it hits the fan. Let's go.'

A VTOL airship was just setting down onto the churned-up grass when they emerged, blinking, into the sunlight. A command car, engine running, stood just outside. All of the soldiers present were facing outwards away from the trailer, weapons ready. As soon as the passengers were inside the car the driver–a full colonel–gunned it to life. General Beltine briefed them during the short ride.

'There is going to be trouble, right around the world, when everything gets out. The UN is calling an emergency session–but we're not going to wait for that. The President has been on the Hot Line to Moscow and there is complete agreement on bilateral cooperation between our two countries. We need to move fast and we can't wait for the UN. The Soviet Union and the United States are joining in emergency defense arrangements. By the time you get to the Pentagon the first steps will have been decided. Here we are.'

The VTOL was an Arachne, the newest medium attack bomber, that had been modified for passengers. There were just six seats in the cramped cabin. The three of them were alone after the general had sealed them in–and the door to the pilot's compartment remained closed.

'Please be seated and fasten your safety belts,' the voice said from the speaker above their heads. *'Takeoff in thirty seconds.'*

Hes'bu was fumbling with his belt as the engines started. Rob leaned over and fastened it for him, and had just dropped back into his own seat when the plane stirred and lifted. It was like going up in a fast elevator. They were pressed into their seats as the VTOL plane leapt into the air, then tilted over to horizontal flight as it gained altitude.

'I did not understand the details of what the large man told you,' Hes'bu said. 'I am not familiar with your forms of governing.'

'He was explaining emergency action that has been taken,' Nadia said. 'The United Nations is a group of representatives of the sovereign countries of Earth. They are slow at reaching decisions. However the two largest and most important countries have agreed to take all defense precautions that are needed at the moment. It is an empirical decision. Do you understand?'

'Yes.'

'Good.' She took out her miniature recorder and turned it on. 'You will now begin to teach me your language.'

'It is a very difficult one,' Hes'bu said, turning and looking out of the window.

'I am very good at languages, do not concern yourself. We begin. Is yours an inflected or agglutinative language?'

'I do not know those terms.'

'Then we will do it in a simpler manner. In English the present tense of the verb to speak is: I speak, you

30

speak, he, she or it speaks. Singular. Plural: we speak, you speak, they speak. That is called conjugating the verb to speak in the present tense. What is your verb to speak?'

'*Kln'r,*' Hes'bu said, with some reluctance. The word had a strange clicking sound in the middle of it, and ended with a rasping glottal cough.

'Very good.' Nadia repeated the word with great exactitude, so close to the original sound that Rob could not tell the difference. It must have impressed Hes'bu as well for he threw her a quick glance and turned away again. Nadia was not deterred in the slightest by the apparent reluctance on his part. She persisted in her linguistic interrogation, supplementing the recording with quick phonetic notes entered into her scratchpad. By the time the craft touched down beside the Pentagon she had the work well under way.

An armed guard escorted them from the aircraft to the conference room deep down under the building. Rob's eyebrows lifted when he saw the high brass around the table there. A number of top Soviet generals, chests gleaming with square yards of decorations, faced their American opposite numbers across the mahogany table. The US Secretary of State sat beside the Russian Foreign Minister.

'I never thought that I would ever see this mob in the same room together,' Rob whispered as he and Nadia took their seats at the foot of the table; Hes'bu went to the place of honor at the top. She nodded agreement.

'Should mankind survive this attack perhaps we can have a future of peace.'

'Touch wood to that,' he said, rapping his knuckles on the table.

'Excuse me, colonel,' an Army captain said, standing behind Rob and leaning close. 'The science staff has been given priority over planning for the moment. Would you and Miss Andrianova come with me?'

'Happily,' Rob said. 'Too much brass here—and not much that we can contribute that they don't know already.'

There were no military uniforms–and no order at all–in the scientific meeting. When the armed guards opened the door to the room a babble of sound rolled out. No one seemed to notice when Rob and Nadia entered. Men in three-piece suits, vest pockets brimming with pens, argued loudly in a number of languages. A slide projector was being set up and there was heated discussion as to which pictures had priority. A tall man, his bald head gleaming with droplets of sweat, pushed through the crowd towards Rob.

'Colonel Hayward,' he said, extending his hand. 'My congratulations. You have done an admirable job of work and we all appreciate it. I'm Tilleman, and I'm supposed to be chairing this riot.'

'It's my pleasure to meet you, Professor Tilleman. This is my associate, Nadia Andrianova.' It really was a pleasure for Rob. Tilleman was undoubtedly the most famous physicist since Einstein, the originator of the Steady Bang theory of creation. If he was heading this committee, it must contain the best scientific brains that could be assembled at short notice. All individualists if the noise level was any indication.

'I've been letting them ventilate until you arrived,' Tilleman said. 'Now we can get down to work. If you and Nadia will sit beside me, please.'

Tilleman had undoubtedly chaired committees before. He took control in no uncertain terms. There was a block of wood on the table before him–supporting an immense gavel as big as a croquet mallet. He hammered it with gusto and the resultant explosions of sound silenced the room in an instant.

'If the delegates will be seated,' he said, 'this meeting will begin. First on the agenda is a summation of our total knowledge to date. You have all seen the recordings of Colonel Hayward's extraordinary penetration of the alien ship. He will answer any questions later. Gentlemen, our task is not to make policy in respect of the incursion of life forms from outer space–the military and the national governments are taking care of that. What we must do is supply them with a complete scientific assessment of the new data to aid them in their considerations. Biology first, then physics. Dr. van Nienes heads our physiology team. Dr. van Nienes.'

The tall biologist ticked off his points with slow Dutch thoroughness.

'We are putting together information on two alien races, Oinn and Blettr. We know far more about the Blettr at present, due to the opportunity to dissect specimens, so I turn to them first. Slides.'

The room darkened and the first picture appeared on the large screen that had dropped down from the ceiling. A startlingly clear, full color and repulsive full length photograph of a dead alien. It was the one they had killed, Rob realized, seeing that the eyes had been shot out. The biologist used a pointer as he indicated the relevant details.

'Two meters tall, roughly human in shape, the body covered with what appears to be hair but certainly is not. Slide. Notice this microscopic cross section of one of these "hairs". You will see a plentiful blood supply here, green, copper-based blood rather than the iron of haemoglobin. Capillaries surround the numerous stomata or openings in the body of the hair. In essence what we have here is a sort of inside-out lung with stoma like this one open to the atmosphere, acting as an alveolus would in a terrestrial lung. The total capacity is, roughly, twenty to thirty times that of the human lung which leads us to assume for the moment that either the air pressure or oxygen percentage on this creature's home world is far lower than that of Earth. Notice this white band at the root of the hair structure. Muscle tissue. The creature "breathes" by moving the structure back and forth in the air to change the air inside the stomata. When alive the Blettr would present an interesting sight, being surrounded by a pelt of projecting pseudo-hairs all in constant motion. Slide.'

Picture followed picture now in gruesome sequence as the post mortem opened the alien and reduced it to its component parts. There was complete silence in the room as the assembled scientists watched in horrified fascination; physicists and engineers are not normally acquainted with the details of the dissecting table. Doctor van Nienes pointed out the relevant features as they appeared.

'The breathing arrangement as well as other biological clues lead us to believe that the Blettr have rather primitive biological arrangements. I do not reflect upon their intellectual capacities–they are obviously technologically quite advanced–but rather their physiology. The eyes, rather than being connected to cerebral tissue, are outgrowths of the brain itself, which is no more than a small nodule at the top of a nerve bundle, here and here, that runs the length of the body, bifurcating, here, for the arms, and here for the legs. Whereas in our bodies nerve impulse are carried to and from the brain by the afferent and efferent neurons, in these creatures the brain itself appears to extend right through the body. The foot, here, would be moved by the portion of the brain in the foot itself. Lights.'

As the lights came up, van Nienes' assistants were passing out thick photocopied bundles. 'We will forego discussion for the moment,' he said. 'You will find all details of the dissections and our conclusions in papers you are now being given. Please study them. We will now proceed to an analysis of the other alien race, the Oinn. Here our information is not as complete since we have not had a specimen for dissection. However we have a few tissue samples, obtained from the chair in which the creature was seated, as well as x-ray and sound scan pictures made from concealed apparatus.'

Tricky, Rob thought, taking pictures of Hes'bu while the interview was going on. He barely listened to the biologist's descriptions now, this wasn't really his field. And something was nagging at him; some detail bothering him, some question that needed to be asked. Was it Hes'bu legs? Sergeant Groot had been interested in them. Perhaps. He listened as van Nienes pointed the legs out on the screen.

'The legs are obviously a metal prosthesis. We don't know if they replace the creature's normal legs, or if they function as limbs for a creature that does not possess any. I have sent through a request that Hes'bu be questioned on this matter soonest. However you will notice, here, partially concealed by the prosthesis, an organ that leads us to the conclusion that the subject is male. If terrestrial analogues can be applied.'

No, it wasn't the legs, something else. Rob couldn't remember it now so he put it from him. But the memory kept nagging.

Apparently the same thoughts had been nagging Sergeant Groot, for just as the biologist was ending his talk one of the guards came in and found Rob, then bent to whisper in his ear.

'Excuse me, colonel, but we have a communication for you from outside.'

Rob nodded and followed the man out. An MP lieutenant was waiting in the hall. He saluted and extended his clipboard to Rob.

'Would you sign here for receipt of same, sir. Message by special courier from New York.'

Rob scratched his name, then took the sealed manila envelope. He tore it open and found a single folded sheet inside with his name scrawled across it. He recognized the handwriting: Sergeant Groot. He unfolded it and read the brief message inside.

None of my shots went near the gun when the thing jumped us. I checked the corpse to be sure. So why did the gun explode?'

Yes! That was it, that was what had been irritating his subconscious. The fact that just did not have any explanation. A lot of things had happened, and happened very fast. But there seemed to have been a reason for everything.

Except the gun. Why had it blown up?

6. Message of Doom

Rob slept for a solid six hours without stirring. By the time he had finally escaped from the meeting he had been awake for over two days. And very busy most of the time. The science meeting had been inconclusive–and the military one was still in progress when he had retired. No one had appeared to miss him when he had slipped away.

He yawned heavily as he steamed himself awake in a hot shower, then forced some life back into his body by turning on the cold water full blast. When he had emerged and toweled himself dry he felt very fit and cheerful for someone who should be very concerned about the invasion and destruction of his planet. Possibly because the entire situation still had a surrealistic feel to it. Yes, the ship was there–and the aliens–but the reality of galactic war still had not penetrated. The idea was just too much to entertain on such short notice. Perhaps something had been decided while he slept. Nadia had promised to keep track of events and report back to him. He sat on the edge of the bed and dialed information to locate her.

Like all of the others on the two committees, she had not been permitted to leave the Pentagon. Rob had been put up in the guard BOQ and Nadia was staying in nurses' annex of the emergency clinic. She answered her phone on the second ring.

'Good morning,' he said. 'Would you like to join me for breakfast?'

'*A capital idea, Colonel Hayward . . .*'

'Rob, if you please.'

'*Of course, Rob. Where shall we meet?*'

'Cafeteria number six. I could tell you how to get

there–but you would only get lost. This is the Pentagon after all. Ask for a guide. I'll see you there in fifteen minutes. OK?'

'Agreed.'

Rob was gratefully sipping a cup of black coffee when Nadia arrived. He pushed a fresh cup over to her and she nodded her thanks as she slipped into the seat across from him. Her skin was pale and she had dark smudges under her eyes.

'Have you been to bed at all? he asked.

'No. There has been too much to do. I have been working on the Oinn language and have made a good deal of progress. The transcript of their radio broadcast and Hes'bu's simultaneous translation helped a good deal. This coffee is life-restoring.'

'Want something to eat?'

'In a few minutes.'

'I'm amazed you can understand anything at all of those gargling sounds. And didn't Hes'bu say that it was a difficult language?'

'He did. But he was wrong. It is as simplified and organized as Esperanto. Once the principles have been grasped it is just a matter of learning vocabulary.'

Rob frowned in thought. 'Then Hes'bu was lying to you?'

'Perhaps. Or it might be a cultural thing about not talking to women or aliens–we can't tell. We know so little about these creatures. But we should know more shortly. There are more of them on the way. After much wrangling the decision was finally made to permit Hes'bu to contact his people by radio. They responded and are sending a ship with senior officers. Apparently he's just a pilot of some kind. Washington National Airport has been cleared and they should be setting down soon.'

'I'd like to see that.'

'You will. They've set up a closed circuit TV coverage here. And I'll take that breakfast now.'

They were so hungry that they wolfed down the greasy bacon and gritty scrambled eggs. Rob couldn't remember the last time he had eaten anything. He poured a final cup of coffee to conceal the taste of breakfast, then leaned back and sighed.

'Everything that Hes'bu told us could be a lie,' Nadia said.

Rob sighed again, this time with little pleasure. 'I know. I have been thinking the same thing. Of course it could all be true just as well. But we have no way of checking. Without a spirit medium it's going to be hard to talk to the dead Blettr.'

'Let me be the devil's advocate then, since I am the one who raised this matter. Why should Hes'bu lie?'

'Why should he tell the truth? We can't be certain either way. Both of us have been trained to look for the concealed facts that will reveal hidden facts, no matter where they are to be found. To put together apparently unrelated bits of information to reveal the greater truth. Maybe that's why we are both bothered now. Take a close look at how much we know—I mean *really* know. Without taking into consideration what we have been told.'

'That has concerned me as well. As you suggest, let us examine the hard facts that we can be sure of. Fact one,' Nadia said, raising her index finger. 'A ship from space plows into Central Park. There can be no doubt about that. Fact two, it contains representatives of two different groups of aliens. Some dead, some alive. One of them is armed, another appears to be a prisoner. Those are facts, physical facts. Not words spoken by Hes'bu that could be true or false. I would like some more of these facts. I would like to know why the ship landed where it did. I would like to know why it came to Earth in the first place. I would like to know who was flying the ship.'

'That's easily enough answered,' Rob said. 'The Blettr were at the controls . . .' His words trailed off as his eyes widened. Then he smiled at Nadia. 'You have a very devious and nasty, dirty and suspicious secret service mentality.'

'Don't you?'

'Yes. That's why this whole thing bothers me so. Something just doesn't *smell* right. The two Blettr could have been dead when the ship landed. Hes'bu could have flown the thing, landed it, put them at the controls–then opened the lock. By the time I had crept into the ship he could have strolled aft and locked himself into the chains.'

'But you were attacked by a third Blettr . . .'

'Yes, and something about that has bothered me ever since. You saw Groot's note. Why *did* the creature's gun blow up?'

'You tell me.'

'I will! You were there during the anatomy lecture. Portions of the Blettr's brain–not just the thing's nervous system–extend into the extremities. Into the feet. And the hands. Do you know anything about micro-electronics?'

'Almost nothing,' she admitted.

'Well I do. And I know that with the present state of *our* technology, not even one as advanced as the aliens', that circuitry could be built into the gun that would directly affect the brain of the creature holding the gun. The alien could have been unconscious. When I opened the door the circuits in the gun could have fired and sent the Blettr lurching forward at the same time. Not the other way around. We fired back as could have been easily predicted. Its mission done the gun exploded to destroy evidence of its control.'

'That is a very far-fetched theory,' Nadia said sternly.

'Isn't it, though. And what isn't far-fetched about this entire matter? And wouldn't this theory explain how Hes'bu arranged everything?'

'It would. And if we accept this theory it begs the question of why this charade at all?'

'The answer to that one is too obvious. To get us to declare war against the Blettr whether we want to or not. We have shown that the physical evidence proves nothing one way or the other.'

'Which means–' her voice was hushed as she spoke.

'Which means that we may be taking sides in a galactic war on the strength of a single creature's statements. And those statements could be lies.'

'Right. And don't say "may". It looks like we are getting involved. And I don't like it. I want to hear some evidence from the other side before we take a drastic step that may lead to the destruction of our world.'

'So do I. But what can we do about it?'

Rob smiled. 'Go out there into space and talk to them?'

'Hardly.'

'Then the next step is to make our suspicions known to our people. Until there is some more positive evidence the authorities must be terribly cautious about any decisions that they may make . . .'

'Look!' someone shouted. 'There it is!'

Neither Rob nor Nadia joined in the rush to the TV sets. They could see everything clearly enough from where they were. Rob had a sense of *déjà vu* looking at the spaceship centered on the TV screen, the same sensation of having watched the scene before that he had experienced during the first Apollo Moon landings. The same scene had been enacted so many times in science fiction films that the reality almost appeared old hat. The dark speck dropping out of the sky, swelling and growing. Then stopping in midair and slowly sinking the last few feet to the ground.

'This is not quite the time to consult the authorities about anything,' Nadia said.

'Agreed. But at least let us get it on the record. I'm going to send an urgent memo through my department, recommending that it go right to the top.'

'Give me a draft. I will translate it and put it through my people tagged for the Politburo. I doubt if anyone will notice it–but it will be there for the record. Then what should our next step be?'

'Get some rest, that's what you have to do right now. I'm going to try and bull my way into the meeting with the Oinn envoys. As soon as that begins, our friend Hes'bu will be redundant. Whether he likes it or not I'm going to see that you have him full time in order to learn the language. We need intelligence. Knowing their language is going to be a first step in finding out more about our new allies.'

'I agree. Contact me when you are ready. The sleep will help clear my mind because I intend to continue my studies conversationally in the Oinn language.'

'I believe it—now get that rest.'

Most of the military and all of the State Department wanted to be in on the initial meeting with the alien representatives. Rob had to pull all the strings he could to make it into the very last row in the small auditorium. It was good enough; he wanted to see and not necessarily be seen.

There was a murmur of anticipation from the audience as the three aliens filed onto the platform. They had almost identical lengths of what appeared to be dark cloth folded about their bodies, unlike Hes'bu who had been naked. Stripped by his captors? Another question looking for an answer. Even more interesting was the fact that they had legs, not metal legs like Hes'bu. But one of them had a metal hand, another an entire prosthetic metal arm. Only their spokesman seemed to lack any deformities. More questions.

The Secretary of State made a brief speech of welcome—he must have talked with them in the drive from the airport—then introduced the leader of the delegation, Ozer'o, whose rank was understood to be equivalent to that of an admiral. There was a brief spattering of applause as the alien rose to face them. His English was better than Hes'bu's, almost perfect.

'Men of Earth, I greet you. I regret only that this first meeting between our races is such an unhappy one. For many years we have been aware of your existence. We have learned your languages from your radio broadcasts and have stood in awe and admiration in appreciation of your vitality and diversity. Ours is an ancient race and a uniform one. It was not by chance that we never contacted you, but rather because of our code of honor. In our ancient battle with the forces of the Blettr we have come to realize that any attempt, for good motives or bad, to enforce one culture's will upon another's is basically evil. We have observed you but have not contacted you, wishing you only good will and hesitating to enforce ourselves upon you.

'Now everything has changed. The endless galactic war has moved in this direction. Our timeless enemy, the Blettr, in their eternal hatred, have detached some portion of their armed forces to come here to destroy you. It is my painful duty to inform you that we cannot alter their course or force them to change their plans. We can only warn you about the future. And offer you military aid and advice if you so wish it.'

Ozer'o hesitated, looking about the crowded chamber. He uttered a small sound, almost like a human sigh. 'It is now my most painful duty to reveal our latest intelligence reports. The enemy is approaching in force. One of their largest warcraft, a fortress the size of a small planetoid, is on course towards your planet. We know from past experience what their plan undoubtedly is. Land and destroy. Your race. They do not wish a devastated planet. Just the complete death of the enemy.'

He waited, head lowered, until the shocked voices had died away and there was silence once again. When he spoke his voice was hushed.

'The attackers are now about three weeks travel distant. That is they will arrive in approximately twenty-one of your days. If nothing is done to prevent their arrival it is the end of your civilization. Once they land you are destroyed.'

7. The Battle of Earth

Angry shouts filled the auditorium. Anger that perhaps concealed fear? Rob listened to the voices, looked intensely at the alien envoy standing with lowered head, but was cold and silent himself. Was Ozer'o speaking the truth–trying to save them? Or was there some complex plot concealed behind the histrionic speech? There was no way of telling. Yet. Rob could only wait and watch. Now he looked at the shrieking men and women and wondered at his own reserve. Were he and Nadia the only ones who doubted? Then could they be wrong? Ozer'o raised his hands, palm outwards, and continued to speak when the shouting had died away.

'My friends of Earth. It causes me great pain to tell you this. I can only add that we offer you all the aid we can. It may be possible to destroy this fortress when it enters the planetary atmosphere and attempts to land. We have succeeded in the past in doing this. Not every time, but we learn with each failure. I will explain in detail to your technicians and physicists but I wish to tell you now the countermeasures that it is possible for us to take. We have a species of energy projector that must be planetary based. These are immense generators that emit radiation capable of affecting even an object as massive as the enemy fortress. These generators must be placed only at one of the poles of a planet where the configuration of the surrounding magnetic fields, what you call the Van Allen Belt, is such that radiation may penetrate. It is good that your planetary poles are uninhabited since the radiation I am referring to is very deleterious to animal life. Your North Polar ice cap is too thin to support the weight of these

43

weapons, but it is my understanding that there is a solid land mass at your South Pole. If you are in agreement we will mount the weapons there. The decision is completely yours. Our wish is but to help a comradely life form in its battle for survival.'

Rob turned off his pocket recorder and left the hall, battered by the shouts of enthusiasm from the people around him. He found Nadia, alone in her windowless office.

'Where's Hes'bu?' he asked.

'Sleeping. Fatigue he said. I think it's just an excuse to get away from me. We talk in his language now and I tend to ask him questions that he is not too wildly enthusiastic about answering.'

'Does he give you any answers at all?'

'Some. I asked about his metal legs and he told me that his people are fighting such an all-out war that none are excused the battle. When warriors are maimed they are fitted with prosthetic devices and sent back to fight again.'

'Sounds reasonable. Two of his associates upstairs also have metal parts. It must be a hard war.'

'How did the meeting go?'

'I was afraid you would ask. It appears that we are about to be invaded and destroyed. At least according to their speaker, Ozer'o. Here, I recorded his speech for you to hear.'

They listened in silence, Rob even more depressed as he heard the speech a second time. He turned it off when the audience roared its approval once again.

'Would you buy snake oil from that man, that creature?' Nadia asked.

'No, nor a used car either. Perhaps we are being too suspicious, reading meanings into his words where none exist.'

'No, Rob. Our basic logic is still correct. We have only words so far—and no firm evidence whether these words are truth or lie.'

'Then what can we do?'

'Nothing—except go along with everyone else. And

44

think of possible ways of contacting the "enemy" where they appear.'

'You're right, of course. And there will certainly be enough work to do.'

There was. Rob lost track of Nadia and her language studies in the rush to get the radiation weapons in place before the Blettr attackers arrived. He was on the liaison team working with the Oinn. Not that there was much they could do to help; the alien technology was beyond them. There were the antarctic scientific bases that had to be evacuated, but this was quickly done. After that the liaison team had little to do other than look on in awe as the defenses were established.

The Oinn seemed to have conquered gravity completely, although they were so busy they could not spare the time to explain the theory of operation to the physicists on the team. Great spaceships, larger than ocean liners, drifted slowly down to the frozen antarctic plain. From them the massive weapons were eased into position and anchored to the solid rock. Cables, each more than two yards thick, ran from the projectors to an underground generating station, housed in a cavern in the rock that had been excavated in a single day. It was all believable, it was happening, yet unbelievable in the immensity of the task and the speed with which it was accomplished.

And none too soon. Terrestrial observatories searched the coordinates that the Oinn had supplied–and soon located a number of objects moving towards Earth. The biggest of them, despite the distance, was so large that it was easily seen as a disc by the satellite telescope located in orbit above the earth's atmosphere.

'The firing will begin within a few hours,' Ozer'o explained to the human observers gathered at one end of the giant control center. A fuzzy holographic image floated in the air before them, and Ozer'o pointed out the salient features. 'It is a matter of the law of inverse squares in the dissipation of energy that controls this. I am sure you are familiar with the phenomena. Since all

45

of the weapons we are using in this encounter are radiation weapons we must take the distance into account at all times. But the target distance is lessening constantly. And you will note that the target appears to be only a swarm of rocks in space–which it is. They wish us to dissipate our energies on this rock debris that they have caused to float before our main target. And of course we must. Penetrate the shield and then attack the main mass. Their fortress has been constructed upon a small planetoid, chambered out and armed with powerful weapons. But upon the far side only. When we get through the shield of debris we must attack the solid rock that faces us. They will of course be attempting to attack us, but we have a good deal of power in our force shield to protect us. They will also attempt to bomb from space, but a cordon of our defense fleet lies in the way. Ahh–the battle is joined.'

As he spoke the words an immense force passed through them, vibrating from the solid rock, washing them with static electricity so that their hair stood on end. There was no visible emanation from the projectors, yet they could all sense the gigantic discharge of invisible energies.

Then the sky went mad. The aurora australis, the Southern Lights, never as dramatic as the aurora borealis at the opposite pole, now outdid anything ever seen before. From horizon to horizon the night sky exploded with flame. Sheets of silver fire that fell and streamed from the heavens as the energy of the weapons energized the upper atmosphere. And colors, rainbows of wavering light that lit the ice fields as bright as day.

Yet the attackers from space were neither slowed nor harmed. In the display bright points of light now could be seen, but Ozer'o dismissed these as unimportant. 'Small rocks, pebbles being destroyed. We have not begun to hurt them yet.'

The silent battle continued for hours, with no apparent victory or defeat for either side.

'It will soon reach the climax,' Ozer'o said. 'They will

have to alter their course soon, refine it. When they do that our computers will be able to determine their probable landing site. We will then marshal our forces for defense. The battle will quicken. So far the engagement has gone their way. We have lost two of our ships, scouts, but we now know the extent of the forces they have committed. You must excuse me.'

Rob felt frustrated, impotent. He held tight to the arms of his chair and for a single, fleeting moment regretted that he had given up smoking. And he wished that Nadia were here to eavesdrop on the aliens. They were calling to each other in their own language now, with no pretense of giving any explanations in English, and there was certainly a growing tension in their tones. One of the operators screamed with rage–it could only have been that–and pounded on his console. Then jabbed his hand, paired fingers snapping together wildly, at the holographic display.

It was changing. The stone base of the fortress was slowly moving out from behind its screen of protecting rock. Now the explosions ceased–then began again upon the bottom of the fortress itself. The intensity of fire increased as well until the entire surface was dotted with twinkling explosions. The Oinn operators screeched even louder now–and the sound was not at all that of victory. Rob understood why when a great arc of glowing white appeared to one side of the projection area, growing quickly in size. Pocked and cratered and cut with mountain ridges.

'That's the Moon!' someone cried out.

It was indeed. And while they watched, frozen in their seats, the fortress in space, despite the explosions of fire that rained upon it, slowly moved towards the disc of the Moon. Then vanished behind it. Ozer'o left his position and slowly approached the human observers, his mouth opening and closing with some strong emotion.

'Looks like it got away from you,' Rob said, his words empty of all emotion. Ozer'o flashed him a gaze that could only have been one of absolute malice, before nodding.

'This was most unfortunate. A variation of their normal plan of invasion. The computer projection did not allow for it. Your Earth-Moon system is an unusual one and they took advantage of this singularity to effect a landing.'

'On the other side of the Moon?' an Admiral said. 'What good will that do them?'

'A great deal,' Ozer'o said. 'They now have a strongly defended base in close proximity to your planet. They can launch attacks from there, provide fire cover for other ships which wish to land. This is not a victory for them, yet–but neither is it a disaster. We must rethink our defense plans . . .'

He turned as one of the technicians shouted out to him, then called back over his shoulder as he hurriedly returned to his position. 'They have changed from defense to attack with their own fleet now that this part of the plan is finished. This can be dangerous.'

This final conflict appeared to be a brief one, over within a few minutes. The projectors in the snow outside shut down one by one and the electrical charges drained from the air around the observers. Some of the operators shut their boards down or turned away from them. None of them looked at the human observers as they talked to each other in low voices. Something was very wrong, Rob could feel it, even before Ozer'o moved away from the group he had been talking to and slowly approached the human team. He did not appear eager to speak, but in the end he did.

'A very unsatisfactory outcome. They had this operation well planned. Their attack was but a feint to divert our attention. One of their heavy bombers evaded our ships and succeeded in orbiting close to your atmosphere before retreating with the others. We scored hits upon it, surely hurt it, but it did get away in the end . . .'

He grew silent as the phone on the Air Force general's desk pealed out a steady, uninterrupted

48

ring. The general seized it up, jammed it to his ear and listened. The watchers saw the color drain from his face. The phone dropped from his suddenly limp fingers and smashed to the floor. It was the only sound in the suddenly silent room.

'Gone . . .' he said. 'The entire city, Denver. All of them dead. A half million, more, all dead. A single bomb . . .'

The battle of Earth had begun in earnest.

8. To the Moon

Because of the sudden war status of the country, it took Rob four days to set up an appointment with Bonnington, the head of the CIA. It was just as well. He had to prepare his report in such well-documented detail that his arguments would be unshakable. He also had to allow time for Nadia to make a round trip to Moscow. It was a close run thing; her supersonic jet touched down at Dulles Airport just two hours before they were due in at the CIA Headquarters in McLean, Virginia. Rob had pulled rank to obtain the official Cadillac and two motorcycle outriders which enabled them to make the appointment on time.

It took almost as long to penetrate the guards and security around Bonnington's office as it had to drive from the airport. His office door closed behind them exactly on the stroke of two.

'Miss Andrianova, I never thought I would see you in this office.' He had old-world politeness and a slight English accent; product of a Rhodes scholarship at Oxford and service in Europe under Donovan in the old OSS. 'I wonder if Colonel Hayward would be as welcome in the Kremlin?'

Both a question–and a subtle hint that he knew full well where she had just come from.

'He would be most welcome, I assure,' Nadia said. 'The report I gave them was prepared with the colonel's assistance. I in turn collaborated on his.'

'Strange times make strange bedfellows,' Bonnington mused, weighing the thick report in both hands when Rob handed it over to him. 'Weighty stuff, Rob. Can you give me a summary?'

'Yes, sir. Basically, there is no physical evidence

that the Oinn have not been lying to us since they first landed on this planet. We know nothing about what they call our mutual enemy, the Blettr, except what they have chosen to tell us. We are taking sides in a galactic war without being sure exactly who is fighting whom.'

'Aren't you forgetting Denver?' Bonnington said. 'You've seen what happened there, that hellish radiation device. Raised the temperature in the cells of every living creature by a hundred degrees in less than a second. People boiled in their own blood, exploding . . .'

'I know, sir. The perfect weapon. No radiation afterwards and no property destroyed. But how do we *know* that the Blettr did this? Once again we have only the word of the Oinn. For all we know they could have dropped the radiation bomb themselves.'

'Do you realize the seriousness of these charges?'

'We do, sir. But the evidence supports our suspicions.'

Bonnington frowned deeply—then tossed the report onto the desk before him, rose and crossed the room. 'You're not the only one with suspicions. This report is the clincher as far as I'm concerned.' He touched the bookcase which rolled smoothly aside to reveal a well stocked bar. 'You'll have a drink Miss Andrianova . . .? Or should I call you Nadia?'

'Nadia, please. A bourbon on the rocks.'

'And a vodka for you, Rob? Hands across the sea and all that.'

'No thank you, sir. I'll join Nadia.'

'As will I.' He poured the drinks. 'Here's to your report. A fine piece of work . . .'

'But you haven't read it yet . . .' Rob's voice died away as Bonnington smiled and nodded.

'Son, it was on my desk as soon as you finished the first draft. You used your office computer, didn't you? I'm forced to admit that we have a few computer taps inside the Pentagon. With the permission of the Secretary of Defense, of course. Alien invasion or no, this department is still very interested when Air Force Intelligence collaborates with the Soviets. A damn fine job. Pulls together a lot of reports and suspicions that we have been getting from a number of sources.'

'Can you tell us what they are?' Nadia asked.

'Of course. Our liaison scientists still have no knowledge how the energy weapons work–or any other of the Oinn devices for that matter. We are investigating the Blettr ship that landed, but have no idea of where to begin because it is so alien. Our techs are afraid to open it up just in case we might destroy it in the process. We have had plenty of promises of aid from our allies–but none of the promises have been fulfilled yet. The emergency comes first, they say. Your report lays out the problem in black and white. But it frightens me as well. There appears to be nothing that we can do.'

'But there is, sir.' Rob broke in. 'That's what Nadia was taking care of in Moscow. We are going to contact the Blettr and find out what they have to say about all this.'

'A little easier said than done.' Bonnington smiled as he refilled their glasses, then sipped at his.

'No, sir, it is not. The Soviets have their big *Musvesto* rocket on the pad right now. They were going to put five scientists and a lab down on the Moon, just when this whole thing started. They say that it will be just as easy to set down one of our moonbuggies and two volunteers. We have the volunteers.'

'I'm sure you do.' Bonnington looked gravely from one to the other. 'What if these Blettr are the insane killers that the Oinn declare them to be? What happens to your volunteers then?'

'They'll be dead, sir. But the point will have been proven that the Oinn are telling the truth. Our only chance of survival in the galactic war will then be to side with them, no matter how unattractive they may appear. If they are lying . . .'

'It is very important to our planetary survival to find out if they are. All right, I support the plan. But why you two?'

52

'I speak the Oinn language,' Nadia said. 'I can communicate with the Blettr if they know none of our languages. I don't think you can question Rob's credentials. After all, he was the first man into the alien ship when it landed.'

'All right, go do it then.' Bonnington picked up his phone. 'You have my cooperation–and everyone else's I am sure. I am getting rumbles of complaint from every department. We are all working in the dark–and none of us likes it. I'll get an official letter of accreditation from the White House for you to take with you. Make you an official envoy. Whatever good that will do.'

Nadia patted her bag. 'I have one from the Politburo. All seals and ribbons.' She smiled. 'I hope yours will be as impressive.'

'You better believe it! Stars and stripes, gold stars, the works.' Bonnington was suddenly serious; the strain showed through for the first time. 'The thought of you two going out there–armed only with some stupid pieces of paper . . . If this weren't an emergency . . .'

'But it is, sir,' Rob said, climbing to his feet. 'And there is very little time to waste.'

'None at all. Good luck, both of you, for what that is worth.'

Although the space programs of the two countries did indeed not waste any time, it still took five full days to finish the preparations. Since Rob had worked on intelligence satellites in space he could teach Nadia how to operate a spacesuit. The moonbuggy was serviced and sent to Russia where the giant rocket was being readied. While around the world the spacewar hotted up. Two more cities had been hit by the radiation bombs, Metz in the north of France and Tomsk in the USSR. Therefore, when the Oinn disclosed that the defensive weapons at the South Pole were fueled by nuclear fission, both the EEC countries as well as the Soviets were ready to contribute uranium isotopes. The United States had already done its part. In addition, many factories and foundries were working day and night to shift production in order to manufacture the massive components for the energy projectors. A number of authorities found it interesting that the Oinn assembled the final machines themselves and only they knew how the devices were built. But all they could do was be interested. This was war and the Oinn were very busy. As soon as the emergency was over there would be plenty of time to make sure that complete information would be forthcoming.

In the meantime Rob and Nadia were doing their best to obtain the single most important bit of information themselves: The preparations were complete, the rocket fueled and ready, the course computed, all systems were go. There were no goodbyes or press coverage when they blasted off. The calculated risk was being taken that the Oinn would be watching for objects coming into the Earth's atmosphere–not anything going out. As to the Blettr; they were on the far side of the Moon.

'What if we are wrong?' Nadia asked, while they were strapped into the acceleration couches awaiting takeoff.

'We'll probably never know it,' Rob said. When he reached out his hand his fingers could just touch hers. They were cold. She took his hand, squeezed it hard, and smiled at him at the same time. He realized then just how lovely she was and how professional their relationship had been up until this moment.

'I'm being very depressed and Slavic,' she said, releasing his hand. The moment was over. 'If we can get close to talk to them they'll listen to what we have to say. If only for a source of intelligence. I wish we could go.'

Her wish was satisfied quickly enough. They were hammered into the acceleration couches as the first stage rockets blasted them into space. They waited in tense silence for an attack that never came. The program had been written for minimum time close to the Earth, so after less than a quarter of a complete orbit they were injected into a new orbit towards the Moon.

'So far, so good,' their landing pilot, Major Koba, said. He was a cheerful Ukrainian with more than a touch of

Tatar about his eyes. 'No bang yet and with every second we are getting further away from their radar.'

'And closer to the ones on the back of the Moon,' Nadia said, still not fully out of her depression. 'One shot, that's all it will take.'

'One shot is all it ever takes, Nadishka,' Koba said, still cheerful. 'And it will be hard for them to pot at us if they can't see us. We practically graze the Moon when we get close, only a few thousand metres up. If the coordinates of the Blettr base are correct—meaning if the Oinn bastards didn't lie to us—we will never be above the horizon from their point of view. And radar doesn't turn corners in airless space. Which is why you are going to have a hundred kilometre drive in that clockwork moonbuggy. I put you down, wave goodby, wait one orbit, then take off and join up again with *Musvesto* which is whistling around the Moon. Then back to Earth, broadcasting a signal as planned so the South Pole batteries don't blast us. Simple.'

'Your idea of simple and mine aren't quite the same, tovarich Koba,' Rob said. 'Now let's get some sleep because we have some busy times coming up.'

But Major Koba had been right. They scudded in low orbit over the Moon's surface, appearing to almost brush the higher peaks, and separated from the main rocket at the precisely controlled instant that the computers had programmed. The landing was smooth as iced vodka, as the major said, and within an hour they had unloaded the moonbuggy and waved goodbye as they climbed carefully into it. Rob fumbled with the clumsy gloves as he plugged his spacesuit connection into the car's communication circuit. There would be no more radio communication once they started moving.

'Are you ready?' he asked.

'Have you looked, really looked at where we are? Forget the Blettr for a moment and realize that we are really on the Moon. Have you looked at this . . . simply incredible landscape?'

'I have looked,' Rob said, forcing himself to ignore the

sunlit silver mountains, sharp-edged against the darkness of space. 'But I don't dare see it. We have to go.'

'Of course.' Nadia sighed. 'There is the war. That must always come first.'

She strapped herself into the seat as Rob pushed on the throttle and wheel motors slowly turned over. The moonbuggy started forward, turning as it went, heading for the course indicated on the gyrocompass. They climbed an easy slope, then over the top and down the other side. Nadia turned to look at the solid mass of the rocket behind them, then back at their course ahead as it vanished from sight behind the hill.

It was a silent, almost dreamlike ride. Dust spurted up from the wheels only to fall quickly back to the surface. One hill looked like any other; they skirted the craters and jumbled masses of rock. The kilometres moved slowly by while the sun hung unmoving in the black sky above. Rob suddenly stopped the car and put it into reverse, slipping back down the slope they had just climbed.

'What is it?' Nadia asked.

'Something. Maybe nothing. If we are on course we should only be about ten kilometres away from their base now. I saw something big ahead–or thought I saw something. It might just be my eyes.' He unbuckled. 'If you follow me stay behind a few yards. Stop when I stop.'

She watched his bulky oxygen pack moving slowly up the dust covered slope ahead of her. It stopped suddenly. Then he turned and waved her forward to join him.

They stood, side by side, on the slope, with just their heads above the ridge.

Looking at the dark mountain studded with gleaming metal that rose up from the center of the plain ahead of them. A device on its summit glowed briefly and they could feel the surge of some alien force move through the ground around them. Rob moved close to Nadia until his helmet touched hers. Sound would be conducted through the fabric of the helmet when they talked so they could keep radio silence.

'There it is,' he said. 'The Blettr fortress. We've made it this far.'

She turned her head and found that he had turned as well and was staring silently into her eyes.

The approach was over. Now the last and greatest gamble had begun.

9. First Contact

'What is the next step?' Nadia asked.

He could see her face, her serious expression, so close to him as their helmets touched. So far away with the vacuum of space between them. He smiled wryly.

'Say hello to them I guess. Funny, we expended all of our effort just getting here. Never really made plans for opening contact.' He thought for a moment. 'I'm going to run the moonbuggy up the slope, until just the directional aerial is above the ridge. Then use the radio. Remote link from the suit radio, just in case. Here goes. While I'm lining it up, you move further down the ridge, among those rocks. I'll join you in a moment.'

Rob used the lowest power setting to inch the vehicle up the incline. He stopped and set the brakes, then stood up and took a sight past the dish-shaped aerial. A bit low. He moved the vehicle forward a few feet, then checked again. Fine. The dish was aimed directly at the black fortress. He would use minimum power; that and the directional aerial would assure that there would be no signal that could possibly be picked up by the Oinn. He had no idea of what they were getting into–but whatever it was he wanted to keep it a private party as long as possible. The radio switches were set to receive and rebroadcast; the solid state circuitry would switch on automatically when it received his signal.

Nadia had found shelter among the jumbled boulders, a good two hundred yards away, and he joined her there. 'Are you ready?' he asked, touching his helmet to hers.

'In truth, no. I don't think that I ever will be. I am not

used to this kind of operation. So do it, please, before I lose my nerve completely!'

'Right, here we go,' Rob said. He switched on the radio, then spoke.

'Hello Blettr base. We are . . .'

There was no air to carry the sound. Perhaps there was even no explosion. But *something* reached out from the black fortress and removed the top of the slope and most of the moonbuggy. Gone–in a single instant. There was a slight tremor in the ground, it died away in an instant, and that was all. The top of the truncated hill was planed level, the remaining portions of their vehicle were smooth, shining, cleanly sliced through. Rob reached up a slow finger--was it trembling?–to switch off his radio. Their helmets touched.

'Short tempered aren't they?' he said, then saw the terrified expression on Nadia's face. 'But this means nothing, really, other than that they have automatic defenses. No gunnery operator, human or alien, could have reflexes as good as that. But machines do. It was undoubtedly set to locate and fire on anything moving, any radio sources. Now the alarm is out. We can expect a more rational response . . .'

The black machine drifted over the brow of the hill and hovered, motionless, above them. It was tubular in shape and studded with bright metallic bosses. Then it rotated so that the open end of some unknown instrument pointed down at them. Rob slammed on his radio, shouting out as he did.

'Don't shoot. If that thing is a gun–don't shoot. Look at us. We're not your enemy. We're human. From Earth. We're unarmed, here on a peace mission. We are official representatives of the governments of Earth. Don't fire . . .'

Nadia was talking now through her radio. Her voice quavering at first then firm. Speaking in quick Russian. Rob could understand enough to know that she was saying the same things that he had said.

'Peace. We come in peace. *Mir.*'

The floating object did not move, simply hung above

them, suspended in space supported by unknown forces. Nothing else happened. When Nadia had finished Rob continued talking.

'We're going to stay here–unless we are informed differently. We're not going to move. Can you hear me? If so can you give us a signal of some kind?' Nothing. 'All right. We're not going to move. We'll wait. Do you want us to do anything? Can you understand us?'

The frightening presence did not respond. But they were still alive. That was a message of some kind. Rob turned slowly to look at Nadia. She was in control of herself now. The watershed had been passed. They had made contact of a sort–and had not been instantly destroyed.

'What next?' she asked calmly.

'We wait. Even if that thing pointed at us is a gun the machine must have vision receptors of some kind. Maybe there's a Blettr inside, or it is a remote and broadcasting back to the base. They've had plenty of opportunity to kill us–and they didn't. So it is probably safe to assume that they want us alive. They must have surface transportation, or other floaters like that thing to come and get us.'

They waited. A very few minutes later they felt a vibration through the soles of their boots and they turned and looked up at the summit of the hill. Without air they could not hear any vehicle approaching, but they could detect its movements through the ground. Nothing appeared–but the vibration suddenly stopped. Nadia caught a movement out of the corner of her eye, turned to look and gasped. She pulled at Rob's arm; he spun about.

It had nosed up out of the solid ground like a great black slug. It was made of metal–yet it was as pliable as flesh, bending and straightening as it emerged. It was at least six feet in diameter, thirty feet long, featureless except for the front end that glowed with a golden light and appeared to be in motion while not moving. When it dropped down flat on the rock a constant stream of small particles seemed to be moving away from this mechanism.

'Well, if not over the ground, at least through it,' Rob said. 'It's a good way of moving about without being detected–and is certainly safe enough. Look . . .'

A panel was silently sliding back in the thing's side. The interior was out of the direct sunlight so nothing within could be seen. It yawned, dark and ominous. Nothing else happened.

'I've . . . always been prone to claustrophobia,' Nadia said in a small voice.

'I know the feeling.' Rob felt inadequate, could think of nothing to say to reassure her. 'We'll just have to get in. We have no other choice. Please, it shouldn't take too long. This is what we came for.'

'I know. Now don't say anything else. Let us just do it while I still can.'

They stood and walked slowly down the slope towards the silent, dark mass. Above their heads the floating machine drifted silently, keeping pace with their movements. Rob held Nadia by the arm and even through the thick fabric of her spacesuit he could feel the shudder as they came close to the gaping opening. Like an open coffin. Rob forced the thought away, fought for control. They had to do it. Nadia halted and looked into the featureless interior.

'I can't . . .' she said, in such a low voice that Rob could barely hear it on his radio. 'I can't go in there.'

'You must. This is why we came here.'

'No!'

She turned away and he seized her arm, both her arms, forcing her back towards the opening, using his superior strength against her resisting body. Hating himself for what he was doing and not daring to look at her tortured face. When her legs touched the low opening she stopped struggling, then spoke in a cold and emotionless voice.

'That's enough. Take your hands off me. I can do this alone.'

Rob let go. She straightened up and looked at him, the

61

terror in her face replaced by a look of extreme distaste and loathing. She was still possessed by fear, but it was overridden by the stronger emotions she had felt when he had physically attempted to force her into the machine.

As she climbed slowly into the dark opening he realized that she would never forget what he had done. That their relationship had changed and would never be the same again. He followed her inside, lay down next to her, looked up in silence while the opening closed and they were in darkness. Nadia shivered slightly, then was still, breathing rapidly as she fought an invisible battle with her fear.

They moved. Smoothly, with only occasional slight changes of direction. The machine could not be digging its way through the ground, not as quickly and easily as this. Rob had a vision of the machine swimming through the soil, like a black whale through the sea, the strange device in its nose parting the solid stone like water, moving through it and letting it coalesce behind. Perhaps it did move in this manner, there was no way to tell. Yet one more incomprehensible alien device.

Had the motion stopped? How much time had gone by? There was no way to tell. Sudden light burned into his eyes and he blinked up, realizing that the cover had opened. They had arrived. He sat up and leaned over to help Nadia–but she slapped his hand away. After that he could only climb out and wait for her to join him.

They were in a featureless chamber walled with what appeared to be blue-black metal. Beside them the burrowing machine was still, the light gone from its front plate that now proved to be an ordinary pitted metal lattice of some kind. Above them harsh lights burned down. A circle appeared in the nearest wall and widened to become a thick doorway that swung silently open. There was a small room beyond. Nadia walked towards it, ignoring Rob who hurried after her. Inside she stood with her face averted from him. The door closed behind them and sudden condensation appeared on his faceplate. He wiped it away as he spoke.

'An airlock. They're pumping in the atmosphere. Don't open your helmet yet. Wait for the pressure to equalize.' Nadia was silent, ignoring him.

There were runnels of water on the walls now as the moisture in the atmosphere condensed on the cold metal. A distant hissing grew louder, indicating that the air was now dense enough to carry sound. Rob faced the circle on the wall opposite the door by which they had entered. His fists were clenched as it slowly opened. He pushed past Nadia and went through it.

Another metal-walled room, but this one contained machines and what were obviously chairs.

Sitting in one of the chairs was the gross, fur-covered form of a Blettr. Ugly as the things had been in death, in life the Bletter were repulsive beyond belief. Its mouth gaped wide, revealing rows of teeth, while the pseudo-fur was in constant motion–like the hair of a corpse underwater. Rob forced himself to ignore this, to concentrate on the situation at hand. The creature was pointing a gun–the same kind that had been used to shoot Corporal Shetly when they had first entered the alien ship.

'Do everything very slowly,' Rob said into his radio. 'Don't go past me or approach the thing. I'm going to open my suit now, try the air.'

He raised his hand and unlocked the helmet. There was a slight hiss of air as the pressure equalized. It was breathable. He removed the helmet and placed it on the floor beside his feet; out of the corners of his eyes he saw that Nadia was doing the same. The air in the chamber was cool and had sharp, unfamiliar odors in it. The alien still had not moved nor spoken; the gun was steady.

'Do you speak English?' Rob said.

The Blettr's mouth gaped open and the words emerged with a croaking, froglike quality.

'Why do you spy here?'

This was success! It spoke English, they were still

63

alive. First contact had been made!

'We are not spies. We are representatives of the governments of Earth. We have come in peace to meet with your people . . .'

'You are allied with the Oinn who war to destroy us. You aid them. They are based on your planet.'

'Please try to understand. They have forced themselves upon us. They declare that your people are our enemy as well as their enemy. Some of us do not believe that. Our governments have sent us here as emissaries to discover the truth. Some of us have grave doubts about the Oinn and therefore we wished to contact you. That is the truth.'

The creature looked at them in silence, immobile except for its growth of pseudo-hair that moved constantly as though touched by a wind they could not feel. The silence lengthened as the Blettr sat, unblinking, staring at them. Then it grunted, a very human sound, and leaned over and spoke into a device on the wall beside it. The language was high-pitched and alien. A voice spoke in return. The Blettr lowered the gun and clipped it to the harness it wore about its body.

'We'll find out now,' Rob said, turning to Nadia. 'We'll get the truth about the Oinn and about what is going on . . .'

'¿No habla Ud Español?' she said.

'Sí, poquito. ¿Porque?'

She continued speaking Spanish, in a low voice. 'I don't know if they understand this or not. We'll have to take the chance. You must know, before you start talking with them, that their language, the one they are talking to each other . . .'

'Yes. What about it?'

'It's pronounced differently. But it is the same language as that spoken by the Oinn. Exactly the same. These two implacable enemies from space–they share the same native language!'

10. The Blettr

'You will come with me,' the alien said, standing and looming high above them. It turned and went towards the wall and through a door that dropped into the floor at its approach. The emissaries from Earth followed after.

Rob's thoughts spun in tight circles. What was happening? What did it mean? The two alien races spoke an identical lanugage–yet they were alien to each other? There had to be an explanation, but he could think of none. With an effort of will he put the incomprehensible thought from him for the moment. The meeting with the Blettr took priority now.

The room they entered now was the first they had seen that was not strictly functional. Cloth hangings covered the walls, woven with incomprehensible, abstract designs. A low table no more than a foot high was in the center of the room, with oversized chairs grouped around it. One of them was occupied by a Blettr whose harness was encrusted with metallic starbursts.

'This is the commander of the base,' their guide said. 'His name is Uplynn. He is a student of your language and understands it but prefers not to speak it. I am Srparr. Your language is my study.'

The commander stared at them, but did not move. Rob stepped forward. 'I am Colonel Robert Hayward, the representative of the United States of America. This is Nadia Andrianova who represents the Union of Soviet Socialist Republics . . .'

'Why do you help disgusting Oinn to war on our peaceful people?' Srparr broke in. Uplynn nodded solemn agreement. Srparr dropped heavily into the chair next to his commander and the two of them stared in cold silence.

'I will explain in detail,' Rob said. He felt foolish standing there, like a criminal before his judges, so he turned and sat in one of the chairs, almost having to climb into it. Nadia sat down as well.

'I am going back to the very beginning,' he said. 'From the time when your ship landed, right through all of the subsequent events.'

'What ship is this?' Srparr asked.

'This one,' Rob said. 'Perhaps you don't know about it.' He snapped open his document case and extracted one of the first pictures taken after the spaceship had landed in Central Park. He handed it across the table to Srparr who looked at it in silence. Then he passed it to the commander. Uplynn took a single glance at it then threw it onto the table as he barked a short sentence.

'The commander asks you a question,' Srparr said. 'Why do you show us this picture of a Oinn patrol vessel?'

Oinn! Rob sat, frozen, while the thought hurtled around and around inside his head. So they had been lied to from the very beginning! Their suspicions were certainly justified. Unless the Blettr were lying too as well ... Anything was possible; they knew nothing at all about either group of aliens. He would have to explain carefully, watch their reactions–and if they gave anything away in their own language Nadia would understand it. Her knowledge was their secret weapon, perhaps their only weapon. He took out the next photograph.

'I will explain why we believed it to be one of yours. You see, in this picture, what appears to be the pilot and copilot at their stations.'

The Blettr examined it. 'They have replaced the control seats with two from one of our ships. But the controls are still Oinn, made for their hands. Do you see?'

'I cannot tell the difference, but I will have it investigated by our technicians.' If and when I return, Rob thought, but it was a good point. He went to the next photograph.

'I was attacked by this Blettr. He shot one of my men.

He was killed in self defense.'

'What sort of weapon was he armed with?'

'A handgun, very much like the one you have.'

'Did it explode after use?'

'Yes.'

Srparr growled deep in his throat. 'The Oinn have done this before. Made of our people a walking dead. This warrior was unconscious, or even had part of his mind destroyed. Within the weapon was a controller, working directly on his brain. Was there an Oinn in the ship?'

'Yes, this one, chained to the wall.'

'Then there is your answer,' Srparr said, throwing the picture disdainfully away from him. 'This repellent creature flew the craft, arranged the attack upon you, locked itself into those chains, It was all a ruse to blame us. And a ruse that worked.'

'Yes, it worked. But our doubts were roused. That is why we are here.'

Srparr thought for a moment, then nodded, a very human motion. 'Your reactions are understandable. But your people still aid the Oinn in their war upon us. You will now tell us exactly how this came about.'

He outlined events, slowly and precisely, as though he were making a military report. The two Blettr listened in silence, stirring only once when he described the decision by the United States and the Soviets to aid the Oinn, and the establishment of the South Polar weapons emplacements. When they heard this they spoke angrily to each other and Rob waited until they had finished until he went on. He glanced quickly at Nadia–who nodded slightly. If she had understood the interchange he looked forward greatly to finding out what had been said.

When he was finished, Rob sat back in the great chair and waited for their reaction. Would they get to the truth now? It was quick enough in coming.

'They lie always,' Srparr said loudly, growling deep in his throat, his blue pseudo-fur waving as though blown by a strong wind. 'The Oinn are killers, they kill us, kill everything. And lie. They are masters of lies!'

'Yet you cannot blame us for the decision to aid the Oinn. After all I was attacked by your warrior.'

'As I have explained, a trick,' Srparr said. 'The warrior was unconscious or already mostly dead. The filth of Oinn use implanted controls to move the body, remote circuitry concealed in the weapon.'

'We had no way of knowing it. We could only be suspicious later as events developed.'

'It is understood. This Oinn, the supposed prisoner aboard the ship, he has a name?' Srparr asked.

'Hes'bu . . .'

Commander Uplynn barked out a word that could only have been an oath; Rob wondered if it was in Nadia's vocabulary.

'We know him well,' Srparr said. 'He is high up, a ranking officer in their intelligence service. They lie so well. With this ruse they get your world on their side to fight their battles. Soon you will be dying for them as well. And in the end they reward you with death for they believe that only the Oinn are fit to survive in the galaxy.'

'Our people are already dying. Three of our cities were destroyed by your bombers.'

'We used no bombers, we have fought here only in defense. If your cities were destroyed you must blame the Oinn. Another ruse to assure your loyalty to them. They are infinite masters of deceit.'

'That is exactly what they say about you,' Nadia broke in. Srparr nodded.

'We can only fight them with weapons. They battle with weapons and lies. For measureless time now we and other races of the galaxy have battled against them. In this time many millions have been killed, many races destroyed. We fight on one front towards the galactic center, but must expand outwards, backwards at the same time. To find new worlds and new resources. To maybe find new allies. They watch us, try to get ahead of us, they have spies everywhere. We discovered your planet many of your years ago and thought we kept its discovery a secret. We failed. While we were readying this fortress to come here and seek your aid, to tell you what was happening in your galaxy, they discovered our mission. We did not know of this until now. We have come to help you defend yourselves, we bring this fortress to your aid. But they come first in the night of lies. They enlist you for help to fight us. Then they destroy you after.'

Uplynn leaned forward and spoke to Srparr in his own language; Nadia gave no sign that she understood. When he was finished, Srparr translated.

'The commander wishes to commend you upon your intelligence in discovering the ruse of the enemy, and your bravery in coming here as you have done. He wishes to know what you plan to do next.'

What indeed, Rob thought. It would take some consideration. He took out his document of accreditation and laid it on the table before them.

'This states that I am the official representative of my country. Ms. Andrianova has one of these as well from her government. Please give us some time now to talk together, to consider what should be done. This is a very grave matter.'

'It shall be as you say. Do you wish to eat or drink?'

'Water. We have food in our vehicle, in boxes in the rear. I saw it was not injured when the car was hit. The food is in yellow containers with blue bands.'

'They will be brought to you. Remain here.'

The Blettr left and they were alone, looking at each other. Rob touched his index finger to his lips and looked around the room at the same time. Nadia nodded in agreement. There was every chance in the world that the room was bugged; whatever they said would surely be overheard.

'Whatever plans we make,' Nadia said, 'they must include establishing some kind of radio link between the Blettr here and our people on Earth, just as soon as possible. We may be accredited emissaries, but the problems are more than just those of our nations–of the whole world.'

'Agreed. Perhaps the Blettr have some high technology that they can use for an indetectable communication link.' He took a pad and a ballpoint from his pocket. 'We must keep a record of this and any other decisions. Do you have any paper?' As he said it he winked slowly and Nadia nodded that she understood. She took out a pad as well and made quick notes as they talked.

'We'll make duplicate lists,' she said. 'Then compare them for accuracy. Our governments must have identical reports.'

'Right. Recommendations. Absolute secrecy at all times. If the Oinn get any wind of what we are up to . . . Complete destruction will surely be the result. We must be as devious as they are. We must establish a communication link with the Blettr and work out a plan of mutual aid. Do you have all that?'

'Yes. But let us be sure that the wording is identical. Let me have your pad.'

They exchanged–and Rob read what she had written.

No secrets. What they said together they translated exactly. But why this identical language used by sworn enemies? First order priority to find out.

Rob nodded and wrote a big YES! on the sheet and underlined it twice before passing it back. Wheels within wheels. The situation was getting more complex rather than getting simpler or clearer the more they found out. The Oinn were liars–and invaders–and some way must be found to get them off the Earth. And the Earth people must also find out more about the history of the conflict. As cooperative as the Blettr were, nothing they said should be taken at face value. The security, the very future of the Earth was at stake.

A Blettr came in and placed a transparent container on the table, along with two large mugs and the sealed rations from the wrecked moonbuggy.

'There's water in here,' Nadia said, tapping the side. 'Perhaps this gadget is a tap–ohh!'

Water spurted over the table until she found a way

to turn it off. Then she filled the drinking vessels and passed one across to Rob. They both drank deeply and refilled the mugs. The dried rations were as tasteless as all emergency rations are. They chewed heroically and drank more of the flat-tasting water.

'The more I think,' Nadia said, 'the more I believe we have but one decision to make. Inform our governments about what we have discovered. And let them arrange discussions.'

'I agree completely that this is too high level for us. Now, how do we call back the Blettr so we can tell them what we have decided? Do you see a button or communicator of some kind?'

'Nothing. Perhaps if we called out. Srparr, can you hear us? Will you rejoin us, please?'

While they waited, Nadia made some more notes–and managed to extract the communication page from her pad and tear it into fine bits and mix them into the crumpled food containers. She had just finished when Srparr rejoined them.

'You called aloud to me?' he said.

Rob nodded. 'We need your aid. Is there any way we can communicate with our people on Earth? We must open a communication link between this base and our governments.'

'Agreement is mutual. Coordination essential. Two things you must have. A broadcast projector that operates–you do not have any word for it–by an energy field that is more like gravity waves than radio waves. We use it for communication. Advantages are transmission of almost simultaneous broadcast and reception across a number of light years. Other advantage is inability to locate transmitter by direction. The signal will not be known to originate on Earth. We use it for interstellar communication, as do the Oinn. Our codes are unbreakable. As unhappily are theirs as well. The other thing you must have is a person to operate the communication. That will be myself.'

'It all sounds very good,' Nadia said. 'Except how do we get back to Earth with this machine?'

'Our commander has worked out a plan. We will launch a raid on the polar weapons of the Oinn. The attackers will orbit the Earth on the way. A capsule will be dropped at some place you direct us to, where its arrival cannot be detected by the enemy. Can you do this?'

'I can,' Nadia said. 'I know the exact spot. We have used it before. All of our Soviet space missions are hard-landed in Siberia. If our radar net doesn't detect us on the way down all we have to do is land near some settlement. This is a vast and empty part of the world. I am sure the Oinn will not be observing it. Is this satisfactory with you, Colonel Hayward?'

Rob thought quickly. 'A perfect plan. I go along with it.' It was a good idea to have Srparr operating out of Russia far from the Oinn. The US would get a liaison team in quickly enough. And they could coordinate all of their plans out of Washington. With these two armed galactic powers poised about Earth any misstep could be fatal.

'Arrangements must be made,' Srparr said as he stood and left.

Rob watched him go and felt a sudden depression and weariness. Physical or psychological, he couldn't tell. He glanced at Nadia and saw some of his fatigue mirrored in her eyes.

'It's been a long stretch,' he said.

'It has indeed.' Her expression was calm and distant, revealing nothing.

'I'm sorry about what happened before we came here.'

'There is no point in discussing it.'

'I think that there is. You must realize that I had no choice. No matter how either of us felt personally, we had to get into that filthy black machine.'

'I know that. But you might have found another way to express your opinions—without physically forcing me. It was distasteful.'

'For me as well. I didn't want to do it. But I had to. The mission was more important. If you had been a

72

man I would have done the same thing.'

'Would you? I doubt that very much, I think you would have found another way. But that is enough. There is nothing to be gained in discussing this matter any further. There are more important issues to hand.' She had her head bent as she talked and was quickly scribbling a note. When it was finished she silently passed it over to him.

Rob looked at it, then nodded. 'Yes,' he said, as he tore it into fine pieces. 'Yes, I agree completely.'

The note read: I DO NOT TRUST THESE BLETTR ANY MORE THAN I DO THE OINN.

11.   Return to Earth

The peasant was weeding between the rows of cabbages with a wooden rake when the shadow passed over him. A cloud, a bird, he didn't care. The Siberian summer was just as short as the sun was hot. It would be winter again far sooner than anyone wanted. And if he didn't grow enough food, why then he would surely go hungry. And hunger in the Siberian winter was just a hairbreadth away from death. He raked at the weeds. The silent shadow drifted over him again, obscuring the sun. That big?

He looked up and stood frozen, petrified and gaping, as the dark cylinder floated down towards him.

'Boshemoi . . .!' he screeched weakly as it dropped. It was going to crush him! The rake dropped from his limp fingers as the thing floated off to one side and settled gently to the ground in his field of cabbages. Before he could flee, an opening appeared in the object's side and a silver figure stepped out. He screeched and ran and Nadia called after him.

'Come back you fool. Haven't you ever seen a cosmonaut before?'

She had a Muscovite accent and the firm tones of authority. Still trembling, he obeyed. Nadia pointed to the group of white buildings less than a kilometre away along the dirt track.

'Is that the collective farm? Good? And there is a telephone there? Even better.' She turned and spoke in English to Rob who had joined her on the ground. 'I'll be able to telephone down there. Keep Srparr inside. This one would die of a heart attack if he saw anything like that. Stay close. I'll be back as soon as I put the call through.'

The peasant watched Nadia start down the track to the farm, then he turned back and became aware for the first time of the damage done to his fields.

'*Kapusta . . .*' he wailed.

'Let's not worry about your damned cabbages!' Rob said, suddenly very tired. The Earth in peril, a trip to the Moon and back—now he was supposed to be concerned with the crushed cabbages. Enough of his feelings came through in his voice to drive the peasant scurrying away. Rob sat down in the shade of the capsule to wait.

He could see when Nadia started back from the farm, and she was only halfway to the capsule when the first of the helicopters arrived. The military here are efficient and fast, he thought, give them that. The copter stirred up a whirlwind of dust as it settled into the field. The blades had just slowed to a stop as Nadia hurried up to talk to the pilot. As she did this a squad of soldiers dropped from the machine and spread out to provide cover on all sides. They did not approach the capsule. Nadia took a bundle from the pilot before she returned to the capsule, to drop down wearily beside Rob. Her face was wet with perspiration and streaked with dust.

'It's going to be all right,' she said. 'I managed to get through to Moscow and they took care of everything. The trucks will be here soon, but meanwhile I made sure that the copter brought this.'

She opened the army knapsack and took out a bottle of Vodka Dubrovka, chilled and beaded with moisture. 'They forgot the glasses,' she said as she pulled out the cork and raised the bottle to her lips.

'Terrible!' he took it from her and drank deep himself. Nadia dug down into the knapsack and produced a loaf of brown bread and a salami.

'It's all they had,' she said.

'No complaints.'

They ate and drank together and Rob felt that some of the antipathy had drained from her. He knew better than to talk about it. By the time the edge was off their appetites a dust cloud down the road heralded the arrival of the convoy. Nadia went to direct the largest, canvas-covered truck to back up to the open capsule. The fewer witnesses the better, even here in the heart of the Soviet Union. No word of the presence of the Blettr must leak out or they faced instant catastrophe. There was a shouted command and all of the troops faced outwards. The alien emerged from the capsule and slipped out of sight inside the truck. Nadia and Rob labored themselves to transfer the containers of equipment and food that Srparr had brought. They were perspiring freely before this was done. Nadia signalled when the job was completed. They dropped wearily onto the wooden benches as the convoy started forward.

'They are very excited in Moscow,' Nadia said. 'I gave them no details over the phone. Just told them that our reconaissance was successful and that they were to provide transportation and top secrecy. We will meet at Base Rozavi. You will never have heard of it.'

'Pink Base. Your highly secret underground control center for the Baltic.'

She raised her eyebrows. 'Your intelligence people are a lot better than I imagined.'

'That's not important any more, is it?'

'No. May it stay that way. This newfound alliance between our countries, it is what you Americans call a fringe benefit of the galactic war.'

'It surely is, the only decent thing that has come out of the whole mess so far. It had to take a war in outer space to show us that our national differences were just family squabbles.'

'It is very hot here and I am most uncomfortable,' Srparr said. The fur-like tendrils that covered his body were waving and thrashing violently. 'Too hot.'

'Just a few minutes more,' Nadia said. 'We'll be at the air base. You will be put aboard a plane at once. All of the aircraft are air conditioned so it can be adjusted to a lower temperature. And the base where we are going can be cooled as well. Can you hold out?'

'Will hold out. Don't feel good.' The alien slumped in discomfort and appeared to go to sleep.

'Have my people been informed?' Rob asked.

'Yes. Most of the staff of your embassy in Moscow is on the way there now.'

'Then you won't need me. They'll set up the recording and communication links, the liaison that we will need. My job now is to report everything that has happened to Washington. There will have to be agreement on the absolutely top level when we start working with the Blettr.'

'There should be no problem. There will be supersonic aircraft available at the base. I have authorization right from the top. By the time you telephone through your flight plan we'll have a craft on the line.'

Nadia was as good as her word. It was a two-place reconnaissance craft that could hit Mach 3.6 in an emergency. This was an emergency. When they reached cruising altitude, Rob dozed off and woke only when the jar of lowering the landing gear shook him awake. They dropped through layers of thick cloud to set down on the wet runway in the middle of a heavy rainstorm. Following instructions from the tower, the pilot waited on the runway until a follow-me car appeared. They ended up on a taxiway out of sight of the terminal, and the engines had just died into silence when the Army helicopter dropped down out of the mist.

Rob felt filthy and unshaven, and he was, when he was ushered into the conference room deep under the Pentagon. Not a word had been spoken to him by his military escort when he had been rushed here. Bonnington came forward to greet him, holding out his hand.

'You did it, my boy, you did it. Please accept my heartiest congratulations.'

'Thank you, sir. But I couldn't have done it without Nadia . . .'

'Of course, of course. Fine young lady. I want your report and there will be one more person present. Yes, here he is now.'

Rob snapped to attention, then shook the outstretched hand.

'Well done, colonel.'

'Thank you, Mr. President.'

'Now I want you to sit down in that chair and tell us everything that has happened. We're making a recording and you'll meet with the committee later–but at the present moment I want you to tell me just what happened up there on the Moon. Bonnington has told me about the doubts that sent you there, doubts that I share. Now, let's have it.'

Rob told them, slowly and carefully, leaving out nothing. Bonnington sat stiff and silent, while the President leaned forward, taking in every word. There were deep wrinkles around his eyes and his lined face set into a mask of deep concern as Rob spoke. When Rob had finished the President leaned back with a deep sigh. Lost in thought. Unknowingly, his fingers took a jellybean from the bag in his jacket pocket and slipped it into his mouth.

'Do you have any personal conclusions about this whole matter, colonel?' he asked.

'Yes, sir. My concerns are shared by Ms. Andrianova as well. While we were still with the Blettr she slipped me a note. It read something like I don't trust these Blettr any more than I do the Oinn. I agree completely with her.'

'I would like to know why.'

'Basically for the same reason we originally mistrusted the Oinn. All of their reasons for the war and invasion are verbal. With no evidence to back the words up. If you put aside what we have been told–just what physical evidence do we have? A spaceship lands with two kinds of aliens in it. Either group could have arranged this. All we have is each side's statements that the other lot is responsible. So we put that aside as unproven against either side. If we don't consider that as evidence, why then all that we are left with is a galactic war with Earth stuck right in the middle. One side has a fortress on the Moon, the other massive gun

78

emplacements at the South Pole. And while they are shooting at each other we have lost three cities and some millions of people. *That* is the reality of the situation. Everything else is, well, just show business.'

The President nodded slowly. 'Show biz. I know a thing or two about that. Do you have any other hard evidence to support your beliefs?'

'The language. Both groups of aliens–as alien from each other as we are from them–speak the same language. Why? I have a feeling that if we can discover the answer to this we will know a lot more about this galactic conflict. As for the rest of my reactions, they're emotional, sir. I admit that. I don't feel that we have been told the truth at any time by either of these aliens. That they are in conflict I don't doubt. That they are concealing from us their true reasons for this giant conflict . . . well I just don't doubt this either.'

'You are making grave charges, Rob,' Bonnington said. 'On very little evidence, as you have admitted yourself.'

'They are not charges, sir, just my personal feelings that I was asked to express. My charges are that we have been thrust into a war that we don't understand and we have suffered heavily already. Those facts can't be argued with, sir.'

'Indeed they cannot,' the President agreed. 'Do you have any recommendations for us, colonel?'

'Only to be wary, sir. To trust neither bunch, to always remember that our true loyalties are to mankind, not to some warring powers from the stars.'

The President nodded agreement. 'I concur with that. How do you think the Russkies feel?'

'Exactly the same. They are a suspicious lot in any case and I know they think that something stinks here.'

'For a change we are in agreement. Any other recommendations?'

'Yes, sir. But, please excuse me. My ideas are very presumptuous and perhaps way out of line.'

The President shook his head. 'No indeed. I have asked you and I intend to listen with care. I shall not

79

forget that you were the first man into that alien ship–and the one who contacted the Blettr on the Moon as well. If anyone can see all the way around this problem–why that person has to be you.'

'Go on, Rob,' Bonnington said, in a low voice. 'If you have any ideas, why spit them out.'

Rob straightened up in the chair, his shoulders pushed back. He took a deep breath–then spoke in as calm a voice as he could.

'Yes, sir. I feel that we can't trust either side nor should we align ourselves with either side. For the moment we must pretend to each group that we want to help them. This should be a cover for our own motives. We need the power to stand alone, power to bargain with, power to defend ourselves if we have to.'

'You're asking a lot, son,' the President said. 'They have immense weapons and devices far beyond our imagining.'

'I know that, sir. We don't have anything to match what they've got. Therefore our first order of business must be to expand our intelligence networks. We must enlist every scientist that we can in order to discover how the alien weapons work. While at the same time we must be just as deceitful as these two deceitful races. We must promise them both aid, and actually give them enough aid so that they don't doubt our intentions. This must be done with such sincerity that they will have no idea of our real motives.'

Their eyes were fixed on Rob now in silent attention. He took a deep breath before he spoke again.

'I suggest, in all seriousness, that we arm ourselves in secret with weapons as strong as theirs. Looking forwards to the time when we can declare war on both of them. Throw them off our world and off the Moon and get rid of them forever.'

The President gasped, for he was a man who showed his emotions, while even the unflappable Bonnington widened his eyes with some degree of alarm. It was rather a frightening idea.

12. Command Decision

The little sailboat rode the swell of the big Atlantic rollers like a cork. There was a fresh breeze that gave it a good turn of speed and Rob enjoyed the smooth motion, keeping the sail taut with a light touch on the tiller. The sun was hot in a bright blue sky that was empty of clouds, the sea empty of other vessels. Off to the west the high towers of Miami Beach climbed like a mountain range out of the sea. It was a good day.

Nadia leaned back in the bow, her eyes closed against the sunlight. She was wearing a black and highly insubstantial bikini and looked very good. Rob put thoughts of that from his mind; they had a far more serious reason for being here.

'We're far enough from shore now,' he said. She opened her eyes and lifted her head.

'And this little boat?'

'Picked at random from a hundred like it. And I've searched it as well. No mechanical or electronic apparatus of any kind aboard. We can talk safely here.'

'We go to preposterous lengths for secrecy. It is very tiring.'

'It would be even more tiring to watch the entire world blow up. We can't let the aliens get the slightest idea of what we are planning–or even thinking.'

Nadia sighed and let her fingers trail in the water beside the bow. 'You are right, of course. I am tired, there is no other reason for this depression. That and the eternal tension, the fear that I will give something away. It gets harder, not easier.'

Rob wanted to lean forward, to touch her, to sympathize and try to help her. He did not; his grip tightened on the tiller and the sail flapped. He eased off. Since the moment when he had forced her into the capsule the relationship between them had changed. The hell with it! There were more important things to be considered than his personal feelings.

'We have no choice.' His voice was impersonal, even cold. He was aware of her eyes glancing towards him, but took no notice. 'It just so happens that we are in this up to our necks. You and I have been in this thing from the very beginning and we will be there at the end–no matter what that end turns out to be. We are here to work. Now let's work.'

'My, how forceful and virile we are today,' she snapped the words, her face drawn and angry. This reaction lasted only a moment, then she dipped up a handful of sea water and rubbed it across her forehead, let it drip down onto her cheeks. When she spoke again her voice was under control. 'Sorry, I'm just being stupid. I know that the work must be done. Have there been any decisions from the joint military staffs?'

'No, absolutely no change. They talk a lot, plenty of arguments, but the result is always the same. Indecision. A clear division between the hawks and the doves, as always. The recommended action is such a major one and they are still hesitant about taking it. They want more information about Srparr. Has he come up with the diagrams yet?'

She shook her head. 'Negative. He says he is no technician, that is not his field. And the details are too complex to be sent through his communicator.'

'Then we are just where we were a few months ago. All over the world factories are building components for Oinn weapons. Yet the vital control circuitry to make them work is missing. The Oinn won't reveal the secret–while the Blettr are dragging their feet and are just as bad.'

'There must be some way to break the stalemate.'

'Agreed–but how? Watch your head, I'm going to go about.'

'That is, as you say, the sixty-four dollar question.'

Nadia ducked as he swung the tiller over. The sail

flapped as it lost the wind, then swung across the boat and filled again on the new course.

'There's going to be a conference later today,' Rob said. 'First meeting of the various research teams. I'll be there as an observer, and to deliver a report from your people. That's why I had to meet you, to see if there has been any progress at your end.'

'Nothing of any technical importance–or of any intelligence interest either. I either listen when Srparr is reporting, or hear a tape of the conversation later. Everything he says is absolutely correct, identical to the translation he gives us. I'm beginning to wonder if we should be so suspicious of the Blettr.'

'On the evidence of words once again? They know that we have been working with the Oinn and might have learned their language. They could just be playing it very smart. Do you hear the other side of the conversation, the input from the Moon?'

'No. Srparr wears a sort of headphone unit. We haven't succeeded in tapping the signal yet.'

'So there you are. His superiors could be telling him anything. We're back to verbal input again–without any hard facts. Is there anything else I should put in my report?'

'Just that we have been supplying enriched atomic fuel to the Moon base. To replace energy expended in this operation. That's all.'

'Mental note made. I have time for lunch before I catch my plane. Join me?'

'No. I mean no thank you. I'm not hating you today, Rob, or rather not you in particular. I just want to enjoy this chance to be alone. To think. I have been up to my ears in people and work lately. If you give me a quick lesson on how to operate this infernal craft I'll stay with it the rest of the day.'

'Easily done.'

By the time the instructions were finished he had just enough time to dress and get to the airport. He wolfed down a cardboard hamburger, then hurried out to the waiting military transport. The flight was a quick one and when they touched down at Lowry Field a military escort was waiting. Rob looked at the skyline of Denver on the horizon. His sergeant driver noticed this and spat a great wad of tobacco juice onto the concrete.

'Can't see nothing from here, colonel,' he said. 'But they're still taking bodies out. Don't smell so good they say. People, dogs, cats, birds, everything, all cooked and exploded and dead . . .'

'We'll get them for it, sergeant. I'm not going to tell you why or how—except that we are going to get them.'

'Nice to hear that, sir.' The sergeant's voice was phlegmatic, quiet. 'Lot of the grunts heated up, want to do something. You'll get plenty of volunteers if you need them.'

'I just hope that we do.'

The trip was made in four stages, by land and air. During the last two stages Rob was blindfolded. Because of all the precautions he was slowed down, the last person to get to the meeting. He slipped into his seat just as the proceedings began.

'I am going to ask for a report from the UFO team first, since their work is of the most interest to us all.'

The large assembly hall was echoing and empty, the few dozen scientists present were scattered about in the first few rows. Professor Tilleman was at the podium and he moved aside as Dr. Lukoff came up. There were no windows in the auditorium—for the simple reason that it was buried in solid stone, deep under the Rocky Mountains. It was part of a top secret military location that the science teams had taken over for the duration. Dr. Lukoff laid a thick folder of papers on the podium and cleared his throat.

'Gentlemen—and ladies too, of course—I have here a preliminary account of what our team has discovered in the alien craft in New York City. A first survey revealed that all of the controls in the operating cabin were powered down, which conforms with the observations made of the Oinn who operated the controls in the presence of our observers. Therefore we proceeded in an attempt to dismantle and examine the various pieces of apparatus. This was a slow process at first since the mountings and fastenings were of a type unknown to us. Special tools were constructed and dismantling did take place. All attempts to test the various pieces of apparatus failed and further tests revealed that all of the apparatus had been subjected to a massive overload and was burnt out.'

There was a murmur of alarm from the audience at this and Tilleman raised his hand for silence. 'Do you know what caused this?' he asked. Lukoff nodded.

'By hindsight it seems quite obvious. When Hes'bu went into the control room a number of indicators were functioning. When he "deactivated the bomb", as he said, he appears to have shorted out and destroyed all of the control apparatus. This would be consistent with his continuing effort to impede us in any understanding of any alien technology.' Lukoff turned pages in his notes, then continued.

'We then made a thorough search of the vehicle to see if any of the equipment was operational. None of it was. However we did isolate what appears to be the primary drive unit and power supply. Both of these are constructed of a material with a physical resemblance to metal but with a number of unusual characteristics. Basically we can't get near the stuff. We can't scratch it, drill it, saw it—or even subject it to chemical analysis. This, as you might imagine, hinders our efforts. However analysis of the power source has revealed that it contains a radioactive substance of some kind. Unless the shielding is affecting our particle analysis, the substance appears to be an isotope of uranium, U-235. That is the limit of our knowledge at this time.'

Professor Tilleman silenced the noisy discussion with his raised hand. 'Please. We will comment after the last of the reports. Considering the nature of Dr. Lukoff's report I am changing our order of presentation and am asking Mr. Dalgaard of requisition to make a brief comment.'

The tall Dane climbed slowly to his feet and faced the assembled audience. 'I will not make a complete report, other than to say that we are manufacturing a number of components around the world for shipment to the antarctic base. Delivery of these components has been delayed because of emergency priorities of transportation. As we know the defense weapons there are powered by U-235. The Oinn report that most of this was expended during the first firing on the fortress before it reached the Moon. Because of this more is needed urgently and a great deal of weapons quality uranium isotope is now on the way there.'

'Don't make me repeat myself,' Tilleman called out over the babble of voices. 'We will discuss the importance of these events after all of the reports are in. The next speaker will be Dr. Heiserman of Oinn Weapons Analysis.'

Dr. Heiserman shuffled to the podium, his hands in his rumpled coat pockets. 'I brought no papers,' he said. 'My report will be a brief one. We have attained samples of every component that is now being manufactured in a number of factories right around the world. Using photographs made in the antarctic base we have assembled one of these weapons. The parts fit perfectly. Superficially what we have built resembles one of these weapons. However the device is not operational. Basically it is a finely-tuned antenna to broadcast on a fixed frequency. However all of the electronic components are missing. They are not being manufactured on Earth so we can only assume that the Oinn have a supply of them. Without these components what we now have is nothing but a very expensive hunk of junk . . .'

Rob's attention was distracted by someone who leaned forward and spoke quietly into his ear.

'Colonel Hayward?'

Rob turned and nodded at the young officer who had slipped into the seat behind him.

'You're wanted in communications, sir. If you'll follow me.'

They had to pass through three separate sets of armed guards, showing their IDs each time, to get into the code room.

'Very unusual,' the code officer said. 'Communication for your eyes alone. It's in the machine now. If you press this button you'll get it up on the screen. Press this one to clear the memory afterwards. I'll be outside.'

Rob waited until he heard the door close, then actuated the computer. The screen lit up.

COME WASHINGTON SOONEST. DECISION MADE JOINT MILITARY STAFFS. ARMED ACTION IMMINENT. BONNINGTON.

13. Battle Plan

There were just four of them in the room. Rob knew General Beltine, but the other two Russian officers were strangers. The general was grizzled and rotund, with the traditional acres of ribbons and medals trailing down his gray tunic onto the bulge of his belly. The young major was something else again. He was roughly Rob's age, hard and fit, undoubtedly a combat soldier if the decorations meant anything. Sharpshooter's badges for a large number of weapons, paratroop wings ... Rob's thoughts were cut off as General Beltine coughed lightly, then brought the meeting to order.

'I want to start by introducing you gentlemen, then I will explain why we are all here. I am General Beltine and I am the appointed control for Colonel Robert Hayward, the officer sitting to my right. My opposite number is General Sobolevski. His liaison is with Major Kirsha Danilov. These two officers have worked together in the past, just as I have worked with Colonel Hayward. Now let me tell you why we are all here.'

'At the last meeting of the joint chiefs we received our first indication of a possible target for combat situation. This came about through a communication we received from the Blettr. As you undoubtedly know we have been continuing our liaison with the Oinn at their antarctic station as though we are still allied with them. They do not know of our contact with the Blettr on the Moon, nor are they aware that we are still in communication with them through their representative in Siberia. What the Blettr do not know is that we are being less than frank with them as well. It is the firmly held opinion of everyone who has dealt with these aliens that both sides have been less than truthful with us. Therefore every communication we receive from them is analyzed and considered from every point of view. I will let General Sobolevski explain what has happened since he is in charge of the communication operation with the Blettr representative, Srparr. General?'

'Thank you. Many of the messages we pass on to the Blettr are designed to extract an answer for analysis. We have suggested cutting off the supply of uranium isotopes to the Oinn, but they have told us not to do this as it would arouse suspicion. We have suggested various operations we might undertake to extract information from the Oinn, and these have usually been taken under consideration. However we did suggest a small operation at the antarctic station. At various times, when none of the Oinn ships are grounded there, the number of Oinn present has been merely a handful, six or seven at the most. Our suggestion was a quick raid to seek information, then destroy the Oinn after questioning, rigging the whole thing to look like an accidental explosion.'

The general looked at the other officers and smiled coldly. 'We had very positive feedback on this one. Srparr was very upset. He said that we must never, under any circumstances, attempt to attack the Oinn at the antarctic station.' The smile broadened. 'So of course we immediately began to plan the operation.'

'Please excuse the interruption, general,' Major Danilov said. His English was quick and fluent, as good as the general's. 'But I'm afraid that you lost me there. Why rush out to do the direct opposite? Shouldn't the Blettr advice be considered and weighed carefully?'

'I'll let Rob here answer that one,' General Beltine said. 'He has been in close contact with both these groups of aliens and knows far more about them than the rest of us.'

Rob nodded agreement. 'I do know them, which is why I agree that this can be the only proper action. We have been working in the dark since this whole thing began. Trying to sort out the lies from the truth. On every occasion up until this one we have always received directly opposed statements from both sides on *everything*. Which means one group or the other is lying–and we don't know which one. Each group claims that the crashed ship belongs to the other. Each blames the other for the destruction of our cities. Each declares that the other is the invader. And on and on like this. If you will examine the records you will find that they differ on every single thing.'

'Except this one,' Major Danilov said, nodding with understanding. 'The Oinn of course don't want to be attacked at the antarctic base–and now the Blettr advise against it as well. Which means there is something there that they don't want us to know about. Which in turn means that we *must* attack and find out what it is.'

'Perfectly correct,' General Beltine said. 'And it has to be a joint operation. Rob is our obvious choice since he is not only an experienced combat officer, but knows both groups at first hand.'

'Major Danilov was an obvious choice for us as well,' General Sobolevski said. 'I know Kirsha, we have served together for many years. His combat experience is considerable, he is a weapons and unarmed combat instructor, and one of the best linguists in the army. He has been working with Nadia Andrianova and is now as fluent in the alien speech as she is. He, and you, Colonel Hayward, are the two people who will put this plan into operation.'

On impulse, Rob leaned forward and held his hand out to Danilov. 'Kirsha, my pleasure. I'm looking forward to working with you.'

Danilov's face broke into a grin, his solemn reserve dispelled by the spontaneous gesture. He seized Rob's hand and pumped it up and down enthusiastically.

'The pleasure is mine, Rob. We are going to pull this thing off. Nadia has said that I must give you my absolute trust and aid, and I believe her.'

'You should be able to do it,' General Beltine said,

then suddenly struck the table with his clenched fist. 'No, by God—you *will* do it! We are going to move into action at last against these murderers, these destroyers of cities.' His voice was low, but so filled with emotion that he had to speak through his tight-clamped teeth. 'We have sat quiet long enough. It is not revenge we want—but intelligence. We must find out which group bombed us, which one started this invasion. We can do nothing else, take no other actions until we have some proof. Get that proof for us and the world will never forget you.'

General Sobolevski nodded solemn agreement. 'You will act. You will strike. Those are your orders. How it is done we must decide here and now. General Beltine and I have agreed that we did not wish to inflict our opinions upon you until we heard if you had any plans of your own. Kirsha?'

Danilov shook his head. 'I refer the matter back to you until I have more information. I know only that the attack must be a complete surprise, so therefore the approach should be by land, since any attack from the air will be easily detected. I have good fighting men who know the Siberian winter. They will jump at the chance to join us in this endeavor.'

'Sorry, Kirsha, but that's not going to work,' Rob said. 'The Oinn base is over a hundred miles from the ocean—which is frozen solid this time of year. It's midwinter in the antarctic. Even if we approach by sub the trek is too long, too dangerous. We must find another way. Something that is subtle in approach and violent in achievement . . .'

Rob stopped abruptly as a sudden idea sprang to mind. Would it work? How could it be made to work? He climbed to his feet and paced the small room, the presence of the others forgotten for the moment. Yes, they might be able to pull it off—by God—it had to do it! He stopped and looked about, realizing that the others were watching him in silence.

'Sorry,' he said, dropping back into his chair. 'But I was struck by this idea. Why can't we turn their own tricks back against them? Why can't we be just as devious as they have been? Why don't we do to them exactly what they did to us? A Trojan horse!'

'I know the original story,' Kirsha said. 'But I don't see how . . .'

'Let me explain.' Rob pulled over one of the large ruled pads and drew a quick circle upon it. 'This is the Oinn base, the control building. Ringed about it, here, here and here, in three concentric circles, are the projector emplacements. However their circles are not complete because here, on this side, is the landing strip. They have some sort of energy field over it that keeps the snow off it, even slows down the wind. So planes can land in the worse kind of storms. Radar brings them down into the field; after that the pilots can make visual landing. And that's where our Trojan horse comes in. A plane. A transport. One of the large number arriving there all the time. Nothing unusual. Only this flight is timed to arrive during the sleep period. The sun never rises this time of year, but they still keep regular work and sleep periods. Also, our flight will arrive during a bad storm. There are enough of those, so we won't have to wait too long. There will be just a pilot and copilot aboard. Our techs will arrange a bad landing, one of the landing gear supports will break, or the thing will go off the runway and plow into the snow. Or maybe the brakes will fail, something to keep it going down the runway, through the screen and out into the snow . . .'

'Genius!' Kirsha said, slamming his hands together with enthusiasm. 'The pilots will have injuries, so will be rushed to the hospital. The plane will contain only cargo, so nothing will happen to it out there in the snow. Leave it there until the morning shift is up and at work. No point in getting more people out of bed once the pilots have been rescued. An empty plane, filled with bulky cargo, heavy moving equipment will be needed. No rush. But concealed within the Trojan horse . . .' He burst out laughing. Rob smiled and nodded agreement.

'You're right. When things quiet down the troops hidden inside hit them. And hit hard. Which brings us to a very important question. When we were first discussing this plan we mentioned capturing some Oinn prisoners and extracting information from them. I would like to question that point. First off, I doubt if we could force them to talk. We don't know their physiology or psychology, so have no idea how to bring pressure to bear if needs be. Also, and this is far more important, can we risk their giving the alarm? We have no idea of what kind of silent alarms they may have. Maybe they even use mental telepathy. So–if we risk taking prisoners–we risk giving the entire operation away.'

General Beltine looked steadily at Rob as he asked the question in a slow voice. 'Are you suggesting that the Oinn be murdered in cold blood?'

'Yes, sir, I am. I think the logic of attack calls for it. And, if we need justification, I can only mention Denver and Tomsk. As further justification it is not prisoners we want but a good look at their machines, their technology. We must find the control circuitry for the projectors. Then, once we have found what we came after, we will have to arrange a cover story of some kind. An explosion, a madman with a bomb, an accident in the heating plant, something. What do you think?'

Beltine nodded slowly. 'Sounds good, very good. What do you think, General Sobolevski?'

'Just as you do. The only weak part is the coverup explosion. That must be thought out in detail and meticulously planned. It must look accidental. And of course the attacking troops must be flown out before they are discovered. It is a simple and straightforward plan, very much like the raid on Entebbe, and should succeed if the details are worked out and followed faithfully. I am for it.'

'Good.' Beltine drew his pad to him. 'Then let us work out those details right now and submit the proposal to the joint chiefs. As soon as we have their approval we go ahead.'

'They have killed us by the millions,' General Sobolevski said. 'Our factories work for them and they take and take more and more of our fissionable material. And we have had to submit. But not any more. Now–now we are striking back!'

14.   Zero Hour

'This seat taken?' Rob asked.

'No, sir, colonel, just help yourself,' the lieutenant said. He was young, blond and getting fat. He managed to talk while shovelling his face full of food at the same time. 'Sit there and enjoy your food, which at this mess hall makes up in quantity for what it dearly lacks in quality.'

Succotash, mashed potatoes, string beans, meat loaf and carrot salad vanished steadily. The lieutenant's slightly bulging shirtfront was empty of all decorations other than his Master Pilot's wings.

'I'm transit,' Rob said, then tilted his head. 'Haven't we met before?' The lieutenant smiled broadly.

'Didn't think that you would remember me, Colonel Hayward. You saw me just that once, and I was on the flight deck the whole time. When you flew into the Turtle base in the antarctic. Name's Baxter, Biscuit Baxter they call me, though I have no idea why.' The fork never stopped moving. As the tray began to empty he managed to slip two pieces of buttered bread into his mouth with his other hand.

'Smooth flight. I remember it well, Biscuit. You still on that run?'

'You bet your sweet kazoo, colonel . . .'

'Rob.'

'I've done that flight so often, Rob, I feel like I'm driving a subway train.'

'Sounds a soft touch.'

'No complaints. Except for the turtles.'

'The Oinn?'

'Yeah. Turtles. Mouths like snapping turtles and they talk out of the side of their heads. Make me want to puke. Like to take a flame-thrower to the lot of them.'

'That's pretty strong talk, Biscuit. They're our allies in this galactic war.'

'Maybe we oughta change sides then.' He pushed the polished-clean tray away and sighed. Then took a chocolate bar from his shirt pocket. 'They just give me the creeps.'

'You're not the only one,' Rob said in a low voice. He glanced around. All the nearby tables were empty. 'How would you like to help waste the lot of them?'

Biscuit froze, the chocolate bar half unwrapped. Then he carefully smoothed the foil back around and shoved it back into his pocket. 'You are not trying to crap an old buddy, are you Rob?' His voice was quiet and serious. Rob shook his head in a slow no, then reached up and tapped his finger against his chest, touching his Combat Infantryman's badge.

'We're going to take them. We need a volunteer who might get hurt, maybe even killed a little bit. I checked your flying record. You're the best.'

'I guess it wasn't even a little bitty accident that you sat down at my table?'

'Not in the slightest.'

Biscuit smiled broadly and rubbed his hands together. 'You just got your goddamned volunteer! What do I have to do?'

'Get over to your CO now and ask for a week's leave. Emergency. He'll give it to you and he won't ask questions. Pack a small bag and be outside the main gate in an hour.'

Biscuit pushed back his chair and jumped to his feet. 'With *bells* on, bells on!'

The great bulk of the white 747 filled the hangar, looming up above the three men who stood next to the gigantic nosewheel. All of them wore army fatigues empty of any indication of rank or unit.

'This is the plane we'll be using,' Rob said. 'You are going to fly her, Biscuit, while Kirsha here will be your copilot.'

Biscuit looked dubiously at the Russian officer. 'Do you know how to fly one of these things, old buddy?' he asked. Kirsha shook his head.

'I know nothing at all about piloting.'

'That's great,' Biscuit said. 'Just don't touch nothing and we'll be fine. The thing flies itself anyway. Now it appears to me that you people don't want a real copilot because you want as few outsiders in on this job as you can. Right? So you are going to have a ringer for a copilot who will be brought inside the base after the crash where he will come in mighty handy. Is that the sort of thing that you are thinking about?'

'Correct,' Rob said. 'Once we're on the ground your role is ended. You just take it easy while we take care of the rest.'

'You can count on me. Not a word. I won't even ask for any food.'

'Good.' Rob pointed at the landing gear. 'Now how do we fake an accident after we land? Collapse the landing gear or something like that?'

'Bite your tongue when you say that!' Biscuit made fanning movements in the air, trying to push away the idea. 'You know how many tons these things weigh! You know how much fuel they carry–right there in the wings over the gear? No way you can take out the wheels and count on living very long.'

'Then what do we do?' Kirsha asked. 'We have to have an accident to make the plan work.'

'Now I been thinking about that ever since you gents told me about your little idea. Let me know what you think about this one. When we're well past the point of no return . . .'

'Where is this place?' Kirsha asked.

'It's up there in the sky, old buddy. Halfway from somewhere to somewhere. The place in time when you got enough juice in your tanks to take you on to where you're going, but not enough to get back to where you came from. So, like I say, I radio in with trouble in one of my engines. Get them worried a bit, set them up for trouble. Get the fire trucks and the meat wagons out.

Not too much trouble, just a hint. Then I bring the crate in, touch down, lift my air brakes and put on reverse thrust. Only I ain't got no reverse thrust.'

'Is that possible?' Rob asked.

'No, but there ain't anyone there that is going to know any difference. Just as long as you make sure there are no other pilots around.'

Rob made a note in his pad. 'That will be taken care of.'

'Right. So we go barreling down the runway without slowing much. The brakes aren't going to stop that thing when it's fully loaded. I'll use reverse thrust when I have to, but they won't know that in the tower. So we'll just whistle on until we run out of runway and up in the snowbanks. Nice and solid. Be some job digging this baby out.'

'I like it,' Rob said. 'What about you, Kirsha?'

'It's good. I was never happy about blowing the landing gear away.'

'All right. Let's go see how the inside of the wooden horse looks.'

It was a long climb up the steps to the flight deck. They entered through the massive loading door that gaped open in the craft's side in place of the row of windows. Biscuit was first in and he stopped dead in his tracks.

'What's wrong?' he cried.

The strengthened deck was filled with large wooden crates, bolted and strapped into position. All of them that is except the first crate that was thrown on end, its tiedowns broken and dangling. A hulking metal casting had burst out of the crate, leaving a gaping, splintered opening, then had crashed into the bulkhead, bending and twisting it.

'Looks realistic, doesn't it?' Rob smiled. 'Made to order. We'll tie it down in flight, then strip the gear away after we're on the ground. One look at this and they will be sure most of the cargo has shifted and won't even consider tackling the salvage job at once. Now look down here.'

There was just enough space to get by the wrecked packing case. Rob went up to the next case and knocked loudly on the rough wood. The entire front swung open and Sergeant Groot looked out.

'All set up, colonel,' he said. 'They did a good job.'

There were lights inside the long and snug cabin that extended the length of all the packing crates. Rows of backward facing seats were bolted to the floor. They were much more sturdy than the usual passenger seats used in commercial aircraft and had shoulder and lap harnesses as well.

'Luxury,' Kirsha said. 'How I envy you all back here. Now let us see the flight deck.'

They went up the spiral staircase and into the pilot's compartment. 'Not here too!' Biscuit gasped, looking at the heavy radio that had apparently broken free of its mountings and crashed into the pilot's seat.

'Realism,' Rob said. 'You'll be unconscious and there obviously is the reason why. No questions asked. So all you have to do is just lie quiet so your copilot can drag you to safety. Which will put the Trojan horse's nose safely inside the tent.'

'Damn if I don't think that it's going to work!'

'We do not think, we must know,' Kirsha said, suddenly serious. 'No mistakes can be made. These creatures have weapons that can destroy our world–if they ever discover what we are doing.'

'They're not going to find out,' Rob said. 'We are going to do this because we *have* to do it. The only alternative is a slow bleeding away of the world's resources. We have to hit them and find out all we can about them. Maybe then we will be able to make the weapons to fight back with. This is our one chance and we are going to have to take it.'

Silence followed his words. After a moment Biscuit cleared his throat. 'When do we go?' he asked.

'Three days. We'll be ready.'

15. All Systems Go

Thirty-thousand feet below were the frigid antarctic wastes, glowing silver in the light of the full Moon. Above the airplane a few streamers of high cirrus clouds painted black streaks across the immensity of the star-filled sky. From the darkened flight deck of the 747 the view was spectacular. Biscuit Baxter, in the pilot's seat, checked the instruments with a quick and practiced glance. All correct. Rob leaned on the back of the copilot's seat where Kirsha sat.

'Better view up here than the paying passengers get,' Rob said. 'I can see why you took the job, Biscuit.'

'That's the only reason. That and the fact you get all the food you want from first class.'

'Even in the Air Force?'

'We won't talk about that. Just got a weather report in from the antarctic base. The storm's picking up. Winds force ten now. Temperature forty below. And that's forty below in centigrade and fahrenheit because that's where they both meet. Don't let me forget to put on those arctic duds before we set down. Storm's so bad they have pushed the protective screen out to meet us when we come in for a landing. Which is even better news.'

'Why?'

'I've seen it happen before in rough weather. In order to smooth our approach they bulge the screen up and out. But when they do this the screen weakens on the far end, so that there is snow on the last of the runway and such like.'

'Just made for us.'

'You bet.' Biscuit settled his earphones into place and swung the microphone in front of his mouth. 'And it's just about time to develop a little engine trouble. Any chance, Rob, that you can fetch us some coffee while I'm doing that? My throat gets mighty dry talking. And maybe a few of those sandwiches so we don't get too peckish.'

As they continued south they saw the weather, still far below them, begin to change. Clouds appeared, then piled up higher and higher. The great aircraft droned on at a steady 600 miles an hour, its sophisticated electronic navigation equipment pointing it unerringly at the polar base. Biscuit finished his fourth sandwich, washed it down with some coffee, then brushed the crumbs from his chin. He reached forward and took the wheel, then switched off the automatic pilot.

'Going to start losing altitude now. Drop down into that crud. Time to tell your wooden horse soldiers to strap in–then do the same for yourself, Rob.'

'Will do. Will you cut off the heat now for the lower deck?'

'Good as done.' Biscuit leaned over and threw a series of switches. 'Left the pressurizing on, and just a teensy bit of heat so things don't ice up. But it's going to be brass monkeysville down there pretty soon.'

'Just what we want."

The combat troops looked up expectantly when Rob entered the concealed compartment. Since the temperature was 55 below zero outside the aircraft the temperature was already dropping.

'I'm cooling things down in here,' Rob said. 'Get into your arctic gear now, but if you're too warm leave your outer clothes unsealed until we are on the ground. As soon as you've done that, strap in. It may be a rough landing. Is the armament secured?'

Sergeant Groot accompanied Rob as he went along the bulkhead testing the quick-release bindings on the equipment secured there. Rifles, mortars, two flame-throwers, sacks of grenades, cases of ammunition. Enough to start a war–or finish one. All around them was the mutter of conversation, in two languages, as the soldiers pulled on their insulated clothing and buckled in. They were eager, expectant as Rob turned to face them. It had been agreed that English would be their working language; the Russian troops had been selected not only for their combat proficiency but for their linguistic ability as well.

Kirsha Danilov finished his inspection of the men, then dropped into his own chair. 'All buckled down,' he said, clicking his own harness shut.

'All right. I'll go over the battle plan just one more time to make sure that everything is absolutely clear. When I leave here now I'll be belted in up on the flight deck. Major Danilov will then take command. The door to this compartment is secured in the open position. These lights will remain on until we are in the final approach. When they go out you will know that we are almost ready to touch down. The landing will be a smooth one–at first. It's going to end with a bang and I want you to be ready for it. When that happens, and the craft is powered down, I'll flick these lights on and off just once. That is your signal to go. Major Danilov will take over then. Major.'

Kirsha turned about in his seat to face them.

'When the light flashes *release* your safety harnesses. You've had plenty of practice, so you know how to do it in the dark. But only the action teams in the last rows next to the entrance will move. And I mean fast–but not so fast that you trip and break something. You know your jobs, you've practised them a hundred times. And you've done it in the same illumination from the emergency lights that you will have to work by when the time comes. Alpha squad will get forward and take the lashings off the casting so it looks like it just broke free. Beta squad will unseal the door from its stowed position so it can be closed after Colonel Hayward gets down here. That is the way we practised and that is the way it will be done. Colonel Hayward?'

'It's going to be good. See you as soon as we set down. Keep it under control. This is the one that counts.'

The big 747 was already beginning to buck in the

turbulent air when Rob climbed back to the flight deck and strapped himself into the Third Pilot's position. Great masses of clouds boiled up ahead of them like hands reaching to pull them down into the storm.

Then the sky vanished and smashing snowflakes obscured their view ahead. The visibility was zero and Rob found that his fists were clenched in his lap. It is one thing to fly, sitting in a brightly lit cabin with music playing, putting trust in the electronic marvels to get your plane safely to the ground–another thing altogether to look out at a blinding blizzard while hurtling through the air at the speed of a mile every six seconds.

Biscuit ignored the view ahead and hummed happily to himself as he brought the big ship in. Night or day, rain or snow, they were all the same to him. His instruments read correctly no matter what the weather was like outside. They were locked into the landing beam which would bring them right down into the cleared area above the runway. He talked quietly to the tower, speaking clearly as he reassured them that the earlier trouble with the engines seemed to have cleared up, however he was happy to hear that the emergency vehicles were standing by.

The landing flaps extended with a whine of hydraulic motors and he pushed up the power at the same time. With full flaps the big jet had all of the flying characteristics of a brick; only the power of the great engines kept them airborne. Gear down and locked. The sky outside was a glare of light as their powerful landing beams reflected against the falling snow.

Then the sky was suddenly clear as they broke through the invisible canopy of the protective screen. The runway lights were there, lined up ahead of them, stretching down into a white tunnel where the falling snowflakes were kept at bay. The bucking stopped as the wind was cut off as well. The emergency trucks were off to one side of the runway, pointing down its length.

'A piece of cake now,' Biscuit said. 'Just like setting down in Biloxi on a clear summer day.'

Then they were on the ground. The wheels touched and slammed down, squealing and burning through the thin layer of snow on the runway. Nosewheel down, air brakes up, full reverse on the engines.

'Full reverse, I said!' Biscuit was shouting into the microphone while he quietly eased back on the throttle controls. 'What's the matter? What's gone wrong?'

The voice of the tower controller rasped in his ears, but he ignored it as he looked out at the runway rushing towards them, then eased back on the throttles. He whistled abstractedly through his teeth as he looked at the runway markers flashing by, estimating the distance to the end. He nodded at Kirsha and winked–then shouted into his microphone.

'We have an emergency here! I can't get reverse thrust. Our brakes are not going to stop us. I'm running out of runway. What's at the end? What? Just snow–well I just hope that you are right.'

Biscuit reached out and turned off the radio, then tore the headset off and hurled it aside. A wall of snow obscured the runway ahead.

'That should get their blood pressure working overtime,' he said quietly, all panic gone from his voice. He reversed the thrust on the engines and gave them a burst of power, touching the brakes at the same time to keep them aligned with the center of the runway. 'There's still plenty of runway ahead, but we'll be pretty blind once we get through the screen–there!'

The snowstorm was back, the powerful lights reflecting from it, blinding them. Their speed was down. Biscuit leaned forward, squinting, but couldn't see a thing. He killed the engines and rode the brakes.

Then the smooth runway ended and they bounced and jerked in their seats. Something large and white appeared ahead.

'Yippee!' Biscuit shouted, applying full rudder and slamming down on the left brakes at the same time. The 747 began a slow skidding turn, going on sideways through the snow.

Stopping with a slow, crunching impact to heel over at an angle.

They were down. Biscuit killed all power and everything went black, with just the dim red glow of the emergency lights remaining. He sat back and sighed heavily.

'You know,' he said, 'I don't think I would like to do that a second time.'

Rob and Kirsha threw off their harnesses and jumped into action. There was just enough light to see the holddowns securing the radio that was supposed to have broken free. Rob tore them off while Kirsha dug a pressurized spray can out of his jacket pocket.

'A good landing, Biscuit,' he said, as he stripped the seal from it. 'Will you look at this.'

'Look at what?' Biscuit said, turning and taking the blast of aerosol spray full in the face. His eyes widened and he gasped–then slumped forward in his harness. Kirsha turned aside and breathed through his handkerchief until the air had cleared.

'Sorry,' he said. 'But it will just make you sleep better. Faking unconsciousness is not an easy thing to do. And the drug also stops you from feeling this . . .'

Kirsha swung the leather covered blackjack in a short arc that ended on Biscuit's forehead. He twisted it as it hit so that the leather bruised and tore the skin; slow blood oozed out. 'Once again, sorry, but our lives depend on this being realistic.'

'Give me that!' Rob called out, grabbing the spray can and pushing it into the canvas bag, along with the shackles from the radio that he had removed.

Loud sirens wailed outside and flashing red and white lights moved up and glared through the windows.

'They're here,' Rob said, starting for the exit.

16. On the Ice

'They're right on top of us!' Kirsha said, pointing to the
side window of the flight deck.

Bright light blazed in from the spotlight on the rescue
vehicle below. The emergency teams were good. They
had started down the runway as soon as the 747 had
passed, listening to all of the radio communication with
the tower as they raced after the plane. They had
plunged into the storm right behind the stricken aircraft, heedless of the danger of explosion of the fuel.
Now they were outside. There was a scratching on the
plane's skin and the tips of an extensible ladder slid
into view.

Rob took one look and dived for the spiral staircase.
If he were seen inside the plane the entire mission
would fail just as it began. Behind him there was a
crash as the window was broken in.

Bright spots floated before him where the spotlight
had seared his eyes. He missed his footing on the stairs
and sprawled headfirst onto the deck below. Strong
hands grabbed him and pulled him to his feet. It was
Sergeant Groot. Soldiers ran past carrying the tiedowns and shackles that had secured the loose casting.
Rob shook himself free.

'I'm all right. Get in with the others.'

He was the last one to the hidden compartment,
groping his way through the redshot darkness towards
the closing door. There was a clatter on the stair
behind him as Kirsha hurried down it.

'One of them outside the broken window,' he whispered. 'Told me to unseal the door.'

'Do it,' Rob said. 'As soon as I close this.'

He pushed through the opening and heard the heavy

door thud shut behind him as the waiting soldiers pulled against it. Small circles of illumination from penlights flashed onto the seals as they were locked tight. Rob fumbled his own flashlight from his pocket as the latches were closed and the other flashlights went out one by one. He found the earphones hanging from the wall and put them on, turning off his light as he pressed his face against the door, his eye close to the spyhole concealed there.

They had to know what was happening outside so this risk had to be taken. The microphone was invisible on top of the crate, the tiny lens concealed in a knot-hole.

'Quiet,' he ordered. 'The major is opening the door.' He watched as light poured in as soon as the door had been swung wide. Kirsha stepped back as two warmly dressed rescue men climbed through the opening, a torrent of snowflakes sweeping in with them.

'The pilot . . . unconscious,' Kirsha said.

'Peyton, Slater, get up there and bring him down,' the first man ordered, pulling Kirsha to one side as the other men pushed by him. 'Any one else aboard?'

'No. Just the two of us. What's happening? Is it going to burn?'

'Unlikely. We're foaming everything. Where are your gloves?'

Kirsha shook his head in confusion and the rescuer pulled an extra pair from his belt.

'Put these on. It's forty below out there and your fingers would drop off before you made it to the truck. Here, these men will take care of you.'

Rob could see Kirsha being helped through the doorway just as the unconscious Biscuit Baxter was carried down from the flight deck. He was quickly wrapped in thermal blankets and strapped onto a stretcher. As he was being carried to safety the rescue operation leader stopped and looked carefully around him. Rob held his breath. The man bent and examined the casting that had apparently broken free, then

107

looked behind it with his flashlight. Then he turned and looked directly at Rob.

He couldn't be seen, Rob knew that, but would the ruse work? Sudden light blinded him as the flashlight moved over the concealed spyhole. He closed his eye, ignoring the floating halos of light, and pressed his other eye to the opening. There were three of the rescuers out there now, moving their lights about.

'What do you think, sarge,' one of them said. 'Should we get the big hook out here before this stuff catches fire? Clean it out.'

'Maybe.' Rob was unconsciously holding his breath. 'But I say the hell with it. No one wants to run around in a blizzard. This stuff ain't going any place. Let's worry about it when the storm dies down. Swing the door shut on your way through, keep some of the snow out of here.'

And then they were gone.

Rob let his breath out in a pleased sigh as he saw the outer door close. 'It looks like they're gone,' he whispered. 'But I want complete silence until we are absolutely sure.'

They sat still in the darkness, the silence broken only by the occasional rustle as they sealed their outer clothing against the creeping chill. Rob looked at the glowing dial of his watch, forcing himself to wait a full fifteen minutes.

'Time,' he said. 'Unseal the door. Groot, check out the craft to be sure we're alone.'

The sergeant moved out silently into the red gloom of the big aircraft. The emergency lights were still functioning; that was all the illumination he needed. He returned short minutes later.

'All clear, colonel.'

'Open it up. Use your lights if you need them to free the equipment. We move out in a little over half an hour.' He turned to Groot. 'Anything visible outside?'

'Negative. They've pulled out. Still cold, still snowing.'

'Going according to plan so far. Now all we do is wait

for Danilov's signal. Do you have the receiver?'

'Right here.' He patted his jacket pocket.

'We'll use the broken window in the flight deck. Drop your wire aerial from that. Let me know when he reports. It's up to him now.'

The medical officer yawned and rubbed at his grubby eyes. 'Nothing wrong with him that a good night's sleep won't cure,' he said. He smoothed down the adhesive tape holding the bandage on Biscuit's forehead.

'What about concussion, sir?' Kirsha Danilov asked.

'No indications of that at all. But I've plugged him into the board and they'll monitor his vital signs at the nurses' station. So my advice to you is to find a large whiskey and a warm bed.'

'Thank you, sir. But I better get a report back to my base first. They'll want to know about the aircraft.'

The emergency was over, the station settling back into its nighttime lethargy. The corridors were silent, empty. Kirsha walked swiftly towards the main base, then turned a corner and met the sergeant who had commanded the rescue operation.

'How's the pilot, sir?' the sergeant asked.

'Knock on the head, the doctor said. Nothing worse than that . . .'

'You guys were lucky.'

'You can say that again. Thanks for digging us out of there. It was getting pretty cold.'

'All in a day's work. You want some coffee? My crew is in here warming up.'

'I'd like to, but I have to talk to my base. Thank them for me, will you please.'

Kirsha met no one else on his way to the radio room. He had never been in the antarctic base before, but he had carefully memorized its layout. The second corridor on his right, yes, there it was. He pushed open the door and stood face to face with an Oinn.

'What has occurred?' the creature said. Its mouth did not move but the opening on the side of its head flapped open as it spoke. There was an acrid odor about the creature, something Kirsha had never smelled before. This was the first one of the Oinn he had ever met; he had no difficulty at all in pretending startlement and drawing back.

'What . . .?' he said, letting his jaw hang a bit. The Oinn showed no sign of any expression as it looked him up and down.

'You I have never seen before. You wear wings. Were you on the aircraft out there?'

'Yes, sir. Copilot. Pilot lost an engine I think, happened fast, out of control. Off the end of the runway. I gotta report to my base.'

Kirsha sidled around the alien, then hurried across to the night operator. The Oinn watched him for a moment longer, then turned and left. The radio operator cleared his throat and spat expressively into the waste basket.

'You get them around here like that all the time?' Kirsha asked, looking at the closed door.

'No. And if we did I would quit. Turtles are about as attractive as pig shit. I hear you guys got out of the plane OK. A close one.'

'A little too close. I have to talk to my base. What's the drill from here?'

'Take that phone over. I'll give you a satellite line right into the military network. Just dial your number.'

It was the correct number for the supply base, but the extension hooked right through to a different phone a thousand miles away from the base.

'Yes?' General Sobolevski said.

'We had an accident on landing. Have you had a report on it yet?'

'Yes. How are you and the pilot?'

'Pilot was knocked out. He's in the hospital. He'll be all right. I'm going to bed now.'

'Good luck.'

Kirsha slowly hung up the phone. *Going to Bed* was the code name of the operation. He waved to the operator and left the radio room. The corridors were silent and dark – with a chill of the antarctic seeping through.

He listened carefully at each turning, not wanting to meet anyone else. If he were found he could always claim that he was lost. But this would delay the operation and he didn't want that. Exact timing was important—and it would be getting very cold out there in the plane. Most of the lights were out in the kitchen; the smell of old grease hung heavy in the air. Silently, he slipped along behind the rows of stoves and opened the door beyond. It was far colder here. A short corridor led past the storerooms to an outer entrance that was used to deliver supplies. He zippered his parka shut as he went along, putting on his heavy gloves before he pulled down on the heavy door handle. It swung open on oiled hinges.

His breath fogged the air of the small room beyond. The last door before him was the one that opened into the antarctic night. He carefully closed the inner door before crossing the room. The alarm was easy to spot; a black box mounted on the frame with two wires leading from it. Not a burglar alarm—no need for them here!— but a signal to the control room that an outer door had been opened. Only they weren't to know. He reached up the pair of dykes and clipped the right hand wire as he had been instructed. Then looked at his watch.

A little over an hour had passed since he had left the plane. Very good. He took his gloves off while he slipped the fur hood up over his head and secured it in place. The dykes went back into his leg pocket and he took what appeared to be a paging alarm from his belt. When he pushed on it the front fell away disclosing a switch and a single red button. Kirsha smiled at it; then put his gloves back on.

The heavy door swung inward, admitting a blast of sub-zero air and a swirl of stinging snowflakes. He lowered his head and pushed out a few steps through the banked drifts.

Then held up the radio and clamped his thumb down on the actuating button.

17.   The Attack

The high-pitched electronic beep could clearly be heard above the howling of the wind outside the aircraft. Sergeant Groot dived for the stairs the instant it sounded, shouting the news.

'Signal from Major Danilov.'

'Move out,' Rob ordered.

The attack had been well rehearsed; every soldier knew exactly what he had to do. As the door was slammed open the folding ladder was kicked out into the darkness, to fall rattling against the plane's skin. It had been securely anchored while they were waiting for the signal, so the first men were on the top rungs even before the bottom had dropped into the snow. The rest of the soldiers swarmed down behind them.

It had been cold in the unheated plane–but out here the merciless sub-zero temperatures pounced like death. With the chill factor of the wind added, it was the equivalent of 60 below zero. Despite their insulated clothing, gloves, face-masks and goggles, the soldiers could feel the cold strike deep.

'Form up your squads,' Rob ordered. 'And keep moving. If you stand still you're going to be dead.'

Circles of light jumped about on the snow, gleaming snow flakes hurtling through their beams. The non-coms called out hoarsely to their men. Rob plowed through the heavy snow behind Lieutenant Razin, who was leading the pathfinding squad. The great tail of the 747 loomed high above them in the darkness as they slid down the side of the deep channel that the aircraft had crashed through the snowbanks. They moved their lights about on the glistening surface behind it.

'There,' Razin said, 'you can just about make out the

wheel tracks we made when we plowed in here, but they are filling rapidly.'

'Can you follow them?'

'We won't have to. We'll make our own line right back in that direction until we get through the screen and find the runway. My men are all experienced arctic ski patrol; they feel right at home in this kind of weather.'

'I certainly hope you're right. Because they are going to be first out and last back in. This weather is really bad.'

'Midsummer, colonel. We laugh at such weather.'

Razin stationed one man under the tail and marched the others out into the blizzard. The soldier pointed his flashlight in the direction the troops had gone, watching as they vanished from sight. But a moment later the dim light of another flashlight could be seen ahead. It was a good idea–if it worked. Rob turned back to his men, realizing it was too late to doubt the planning in any way now. They were committed. A line of the Siberian soldiers should now stretch out from the plane to the unseen runway, their lights guiding the rest of the men to safety.

But was the line of soldiers going in the right direction? Compasses were unworkable here at the South Pole. The operation depended upon the lieutenant's experience and sense of direction. He had better be right or they would all soon be frozen to death long before they reached the base.

The great bulk of Sergeant Groot loomed up out of the darkness behind Rob. 'Plane's empty, colonel. Troops formed up, all present and accounted for.'

'All right, start them out. Lights out as soon as they get past the plane and no talking. The only lights I want to see are those of the guides.'

Silently the men moved out, leaning into the screaming wind. Rob stayed there until the last of them had moved by, then swung his flashlight in a quick circle before following after them.

The night was dark, cold, deadly. Rob stumbled

113

through the snow and could see nothing. He fought down the panic that threatened to rise and engulf him. He had to be going in the right direction. There it was! A dim point of light glowing in the engulfing black. He pressed on towards it and found a solitary soldier standing motionless behind the plane. When Rob stumbled up he swung his light and pointed it out into the darkness. There was nothing visible out there.

Rob was about to say something when a dim light appeared, then vanished again. The soldier must have known what Rob was feeling. 'The light to guide you is there. Do not worry about it. It was just the men in between blocking the light. It happens once in awhile. If it does you must stand and not move until you can see it again. You go now, sir. I have to wait for Lieutenant Razin.'

Rob started to speak, but could think of nothing to say. He had approved this part of the plan. Razin would retrace the path back to the aircraft, then assemble his men one at a time as he retraced his tracks a third time. If there were any stragglers his experienced winter troopers would find them.

'All right, soldier. Well done.' Rob moved out towards the spot of light in the darkness, glad that he was not the one chosen to remain here, alone, waiting for his officer.

It was hard slogging, pushing through the snow. If the squads of men who had gone by here had left any trail he was not aware of it. The screaming blizzard had filled in their footsteps even as they had passed. He came to the spot of light which resolved itself into a flashlight held by a silent soldier up to his knees in snow. Rob blinked into the darkness for the next light. There it was. Move on.

Somewhere in this endless nightmare Rob stumbled, falling face first into the snow. As he was struggling to rise he felt a strong hand under his arm, helping him to his feet.

'It's not far, soldier,' a familiar voice said. 'Just follow the lights.'

114

'Is that you, lieutenant?'

'Colonel Hayward? Yes, sir. Everything going according to schedule. We hit the runway right on the button. The men are forming up there, just this side of the barrier. Couldn't be better, sir. I'm drawing in my men now; we should be there just about the time you are.'

He meant it too, charging off into the darkness. Experience. Rob pressed on until he became aware of a stamping mass of men ahead, outlined against the landing light of the runway. He moved up and took charge.

'Just about five paces more,' Sergeant Groot said. 'It's just like a curtain. The storm ends. All the snow and wind are on this side.'

'How clear is it?'

'Perfect. You can see the runway lights stretching right away out of sight. And the lights of the base.'

'I'll take a look. Let me know as soon as Razin and his men are back.'

Groot was right. An invisible barrier stretched from the ground up into the sky. He stepped through it and instantly felt the difference in temperature when the wind died away. The ramp and hangars were clearly visible, about two miles away, with the silver forms of the cargo planes drawn up in ranks before them. Beyond them were the lights of the base. He turned as a figure came through the barrier behind him, brushing away a coating of snowflakes.

'We are all here, sir,' Lieutenant Razin said. 'One of your men fell and lost his goggles. We brought him in, tied a scarf over his eyes. We'll know his condition when we get inside the base.'

'We expected worse. Have two of Delta squad assigned to him. Bring him in after we hit the base. Do you see it there?'

'Yes, colonel.'

'We'll go the longest way around. Skirting this barrier. I'll lead the way. For the last approach we'll stay on the weather side of the barrier for cover. I was hoping we would come across one of the projectors, but

115

I don't see any of them between us and the target.'

'They must all be further out, beyond the barrier and hidden by the storm.'

'Any idea how to find one of them?'

'Done easily. My men will extend in a line stretching inward from the barrier. We'll find one that way.'

'Let me know as soon as you do.'

'Yes, sir.'

'Let's go.'

They marched through the darkness, avoiding the runway and taxiway lights, disappearing back into the blizzard when they were close to the base in order to approach it unseen. They were directly in line with it when one of Razin's arctic ski patrolmen hurried up to Rob's side.

'Message from Lieutenant Razin, colonel. Projector located. I can take you to it.'

'Right.' Groot appeared at his side. 'Get Epsilon squad, the techs, and follow me.'

The snow-covered bulk loomed up, higher than they were. Rob brushed away the snow over the junction box. 'Strip it down,' he ordered. 'You know how it has to be done.'

They were already putting the portable cover over the device as he left. They had practised dismantling one of the Oinn projectors in a deep freeze locker; they knew what to do. They would find the projection and control circuitry, which was half the reason they were here. The other half was the base. That was next. The soldiers were waiting silently in the snow when he reappeared. They were ready. He looked at them and nodded–then issued his commands.

'Alpha squad, with me. The rest of you wait here. We hit the base at that entrance there, secure it. You'll get my signal when it's clear.'

They went in fast, running, weapons ready. As they came to the door it swung open and Major Danilov waved them inside. Rob stepped aside as the men ran by him, turning and blinking his light into the darkness. Waiting until the dark wave of men appeared out of the night.

116

No commands were spoken–none needed to be. Every step of the action had been carefully planned and rehearsed countless times.

'Anything to report?' Rob asked Danilov.

'Negative. Everything's quiet. No suspicions aroused. The corridors are empty.'

'Right.' Rob pressed his stop watch as the last soldiers hurried by. He looked at the two squads of silent men spread out behind him through the large kitchen. 'We allow three minutes for the radio room team to shut down communications. Then we hit our target.' He walked over and stood before the expectant, armed men–then pointed to a corporal in the front rank.

'You. What do you do when you see a Oinn?'

'Kill it, sir!' He snapped the answer as he raised his silenced rifle, flicking the safety on and off quickly. Then he added in a quiet voice, 'I'm from Denver, colonel.'

'One of the reasons you were chosen, son.' He pointed to the others in the squad. 'There are men here from Tomsk for the same reason. I don't want a single shot fired by accident. I don't want a single human being harmed–unless you have to go through him to get an Oinn. Now–let's go.'

They were quiet, moving swiftly through the corridors on their rubber-soled boots. Assembling outside the entrance to the Oinn control center. Waiting, expectantly, every eye on Rob as he looked at his watch.

The seconds flicked by. He raised his hand slowly–then chopped it down.

'Go!'

18. Killing Ground

The door was hurled wide and the men charged through it.

The lights were dim and at first they could see no one. They spread out, guns ready. An Oinn who had been concealed by a bank of instruments suddenly appeared. Rob was swinging up his gun when there was the rapid slapping sound of muffled firing from behind him and the alien went over and down.

They ran on. Another Oinn appeared, screeching something–but as the first sound emerged he spun about and fell, torn and bleeding from a dozen wounds. Then the soldiers spread out and searched the large chamber, the muzzles of their guns sniffing the air like hungry dogs.

'Empty.' Groot reported. 'Just the two of them here.'

'That means there are five more of them,' Rob said. 'Move it out. Search through their quarters. I want the five of them dead. Let's go.'

It wasn't war, it was butchery. Slaughter without mercy. Any pity these men might have felt towards the Oinn was carefully bottled up and forgotten. They had orders to murder–and they did. They had good reasons for the bloodshed, but good or no they kept their emotions sealed away and worked like killing machines.

They spread out, searching. Rob jumped into a room, found it empty, then emerged behind the first wave. They were going down the corridor ahead of him. In the distance there was the distinct fluttering sound of a gun firing–followed by a great crashing sound of breaking glass. They were for it now!

A door sprang open ahead of Rob and an Oinn ran out, turned to face him. Barehanded, mouth gaping open.

'Colonel Hayward . . .' it said.

Rob recognized him. The first one.

'Hes'bu,' he said, the name punctuated by the flat hammering of his .45. Jumping in his hand, emptying. Hes'bu's body jerking with every shot. Bending forward, falling.

Rob stood a moment, looking down at the silent body on the floor before him. Then he stepped over it and moved on into the large room at the end of the corridor. The frigid antarctic wind was blowing in through the broken thermal glass windows here. A crumpled Oinn lay below the window covered with splinters of glass. Sergeant Groot was bent over a soldier who lay sprawled on the floor. He stood as Rob came up.

'I heard firing behind us in the hall, colonel. Was that you?'

'Yes. Got one.'

'That's number seven then. All down. Situation clear.'

Rob looked down at the staring eyes of the dead soldier. His chest had been burnt away, his parka was still smoldering.

'Only casualty,' Groot said in a quiet voice. 'The thing bushwacked him. He got off almost a full clip. Took out the Oinn and the window behind it. But he must have been dead before he pulled the trigger.'

'That's it then.' As he spoke the words Rob felt completely drained of energy; he ignored the sensation and straightened up. 'We'll set up HQ back in the control room. Get the bodies in there as well. I want reports from every squad. Move it.'

It had worked! Rob didn't let himself feel the elation until he had heard all the reports. The radios had been silenced. The Oinn had been hit hard. None of them had reached any kind of instrument that might have been a communicator. And the attackers had suffered only the one casualty. When the reports were complete Rob went to the radio room where their own operator had hooked through to control on a scrambled line. Rob dropped into the chair and picked up the handset.

'Hayward here.'

'Report.' It was General Beltine's voice. 'General Sobolevski is on the line as well.'

'Complete success. Seven targets. All taken out before they could communicate. The entire base is sealed.'

'Congratulations! A job well done. Any intelligence information yet?'

'Negative. The outside team is still working and hasn't reported back. Following instructions we are touching none of the Oinn equipment inside here until the backup teams arrive. What is their status?'

'They are airborne and on schedule. Should be landing at the field there in about fifteen minutes.'

'I'll begin loading the base personnel here as soon as the planes come in. We'll have everyone evacuated by the time the science teams finish their job.'

'You've done a good job so far. We'll report what has happened upstairs. This line will stay open until we hear from you on the next phase of the operation.'

Rob put the phone down and took a deep breath. First step accomplished. But they had to get out of this clean, without a trace of what they had done, if the whole thing weren't to come down around their ears.

'Cup of coffee, sir,' the voice said. Rob blinked at the steaming container that the radio operator was holding out to him.

'By God, yes! What an idea . . .'

He had taken a single scalding sip when the messenger burst into the room.

'Tech team is back, colonel.'

The container hit the floor and splattered as Rob went out the door. In the control room the group of men, still dripping with melted snow, turned as he came in. The captain in command stepped forward.

'You have it?' Rob asked.

'No, sir. There was nothing there.'

'I don't think I understand you.'

'Nothing. Just that, Colonel Hayward,' he said in a bewildered voice.

'What do you mean?!'

'We don't understand it ourselves, sir. We opened the thing up all right, no problem. Just like the assemblies from the factories we have been working on. But there was nothing inside. No signal generator in the projector itself, or any circuitry in the control box. Just a junction where the incoming wire led out to the next projector. It stopped us, colonel, didn't make sense. Instead of coming back then–that's what took the time–we tracked the wire to the next projector. Same thing there. Nothing. Empty.'

'You mean those things–they're just *dummies?*'

'The ones we examined certainly were. Just chunks of metal. I'd like permission to look at some more of them. Lieutenant Razin and his men have found the next circle of projectors. Maybe we'll have better luck there.'

'And maybe you won't . . .' Rob dropped into the nearest chair, pushing this discovery around inside his head. Dummies? But he had seen the projectors fire–or had he? He looked up and realized that the tech team was still waiting for orders.

'Yes. Open two more. Just two. But stop then and report back to me as soon as that is done.'

He was barely aware of the men leaving. What did this mean? What had he really seen that day when the Oinn were theoretically fighting off the Blettr fleet? He had seen machines, heard the battle reports come in, then had seen the holograph projection of the battle. Felt the projectors fire and had seen the incredible effect they had had on the Southern Lights. . . .

'Why–the dirty bastards!' he said aloud, with sudden realization. 'They've done it again!'

Rob sat there in silence, weighing up the facts one by one, unaware of the bustle around him. He was only drawn back to the present when he heard his name spoken. It was Sergeant Groot.

'The planes have landed, colonel. Taxiing up to the terminal now.'

'Good. As soon as they are refueled I want everyone from this base boarded on the number one craft. With the exception of the tower operators. And all of our men are to go as well except for the Alpha, Beta and Delta squads. As soon as they are all aboard the plane is to take off. What about the Oinn bodies?'

'All together in their own area.'

'Good. I want you to personally bring the civilian team here as soon as they are out of the plane.'

There were a dozen men in the science team, led by Professor Tilleman and the chairman of the UFO team, Dr. Lukoff. They were practically rubbing their hands with pleasure when they entered the control room. They opened their tool and instrument chests but Rob stopped them before they could touch any of the apparatus.

'Please listen. Use gloves when you are dismantling the Oinn devices. If you do have to touch anything with your bare hands be sure and wipe it clean of fingerprints when you are through. Take apart only what you are sure you can reassemble . . .'

'We know all this, colonel,' Lukoff interrupted. 'We have been well briefed.'

'Good. You are now being briefed again. This is a military operation and we are on a tight schedule. You have exactly one hour to complete your part of this operation. So in one half an hour you will begin reassembly. No parts or units are to be left out when you put things back together again. We want no trace of your presence here. When you are done this entire area will be destroyed by explosions. Now begin. Professor Tilleman, may I see you?'

'This is wonderful, wonderful,' Tilleman said, watching as the technicians tackled the alien devices.

'We have discovered some highly important facts already,' Rob said. 'My tech team has already dismantled one of the large beam projectors.'

'That's a very good news. Where are the electronic units?'

'Nowhere. They don't exist. The projectors are dummies, empty of any circuitry.'

Tilleman blinked rapidly, then shook his head in bewilderment. 'I'm not sure that I understand.'

'I think that we have been tricked again. I put it to you that the battle we witnessed here was just a show. The projectors are dummies, so they could not have fired. The effect we felt in our bodies could have been just that. A special effect. Just like the device that made the Southern Lights go wild. A magnetic projector of some kind, I don't know.'

'It can't be possible, the whole thing can't be a fake. You were on the Moon yourself and saw the Blettr fortress there.'

'I did. So it arrived, we saw that. But was there a battle to prevent it arriving–or did the Oinn just fake that to get our cooperation? We have been told so many lies, seen so many lies acted out, that we have no idea of where the truth lies now.'

'No . . . we don't. So it is even more imperative now that we get into these machines and find out what makes them tick. We will need more time . . .'

'Impossible. The schedule is tight.'

'It can be stretched a little I am sure.'

Rob's answer was grim. 'It can't–because you don't know what happened before you arrived. We have killed all of the Oinn who were stationed here . . .' He ignored Tilleman's gasp of horror and continued. 'This must never be found out or the whole world may go the way Denver went. All personnel are being evacuated, so they won't be able to describe what really happened. As soon as you are away my team will blow up the Oinn, their machinery and their corpses. This will be blamed upon one man, one of our own who was killed in action. The cover story is that he hid aboard one of the cargo planes, caused it to crash and burn. That is being taken care of now. He went berserk. Destroyed the Oinn and was killed by them. The damage will be so great that the entire base had to be evacuated. When the Oinn get here they will find only my team, all of them drilled in the cover story. Do you understand now why we have no time to waste?'

'The entire thing–it's madness. The risk . . .!'

'Perhaps. But it has been done. It is too late to cry over

spilt milk. All we can do now is follow through and hope it works out as planned.'

Rob turned to Sergeant Groot who had entered the control room at a fast trot. 'First plane is loaded and away, colonel,' Groot reported. 'Taxiing out to the runway now.'

'Good. The explosive charges?'

'In position. Being fused and wired at this moment.'

'Then we're all set. The planned operation is going to work after all . . .'

Major Danilov burst through the door. 'Trouble,' he called out. 'The lead aircraft cannot take off. It is halted on the runway.'

'Why?' Rob asked. suddenly gripped by an inexplicable fear.

'Look!'

He jumped to the window and froze as he looked out.

There was the runway, its row of lights stretching away into the distance. A 747 stood at one end of it. The engines were running, sheets of snow blew out behind it from the jet blasts. But it was not moving. The reason why was obvious.

The great black form of an Oinn space cruiser had settled down before it, blocking the runway.

19. No Way Out

Disaster!

Rob did nothing, said nothing. Just stood there, frozen, and looked at the alien craft for long seconds–before he wheeled about and stabbed his fingers at the others.

'We have to improvise. Any suggestions?'

He waited as the silence stretched out. One, two, three seconds. Nothing. He had to do it himself.

'All right. First, reassemble the equipment–no, don't bother, we have no time for that. Everyone out of here. Major, you know this base. Move these people on the double and get them out of sight somewhere. *Now!*' He whirled on Groot and stabbed at him with his finger. 'Blow this place–just as soon as you can. Blast all of the Oinn bodies and all their machinery. I want no trace of our being here. Just that single body of the soldier who will be blamed for doing the entire job.'

Would it work? He didn't know. But he knew that he had to try. The disaster that would occur if they failed did not bear thinking about. The Oinn–what were they doing? He jumped back to the window. The scene had not changed. The aircraft stood at the end of the runway. The spaceship, ports still closed, blocking its takeoff.

'Ready to blow,' Sergeant Groot reported.

'Let's go. Fire as soon as we're clear. Then get some transportation and meet me at the terminal exit.'

They ran. Rob was just entering the radio room when the explosion shook the building, almost knocking him from his feet. A shower of dust came down from the ceiling.

The radio operator turned to him, frightened. 'What's that . . .'

'Silence. Call the tower. Tell them to get that plane off the runway and back into the terminal.' He grabbed up the phone. 'General?'

'*I'm here and . . .*'

'Big trouble, sir. An Oinn ship has landed. The planes haven't left yet. We've blown up the evidence. I'm going out to the Oinn now. I'm going to try and sell them a new story. Keep everything buttoned tight at your end.'

He slammed down the phone before the general had a chance to answer. Major Danilov was in the hallway outside.

'The scientists are out of sight,' the major said. 'But everyone left on the base knows what happened. If the Oinn talk to them . . .'

'We've got to stop them, head them off. Come out to their ship with me. We have to find a way of making sure that they don't get in here until we are ready for them.'

'Shall I take a squad?'

'Armed support?' Rob stopped to think. 'Yes. Might be a good idea. We can't use force against them–but let them see that we mean it. That there is danger here and that we are protecting them. I must convince them that it's for their own safety. Keep them in the ship. Get your men.'

Sergeant Groot had one of the personnel transporters waiting at the terminal. This was a modified 5-ton truck, insulated and fitted with benches inside. Rob pointed to it. 'Major, get your men inside. Stay low as you board. Keep the body of the truck between them and the ship in case we're under surveillance. They are to keep down and keep quiet, out of sight. You'll ride up front with me. Let's go.'

The truck was warm, stored in a heated garage, and the big blower soon dispelled the chill that had poured in through the open door. They passed the 747 as it was returning to the terminal. Then there was nothing between them and the bulk of the alien ship.

'Looks like a hatch is opening,' Kirsha said.

'Floor it,' Rob ordered. 'Stop so your open door faces that entrance. Keep your weapon close. The major and I will go out and talk. Our hands will be empty but we need to show them your gun in order to make a point.'

The door was open as the truck skidded to a halt, just in front of the two Oinn, dressed in heavy wrappings, who had just stepped through the open port. Rob swung down with Kirsha right behind him. He recognized the lead figure. Ozer'o, the commander of the delegation on Earth.

'There has been some trouble . . .' Rob said, but Ozer'o interrupted him.

'We received an emergency alarm from this base. But we cannot contact our people. We saw an explosion. You will explain as you transport us to the base.'

'I said there has been trouble. The base was attacked. Terrorists, we don't know how many. We have troops in there cleaning them out . . .'

'Take us now.' He moved forward with the second Oinn in step behind him. Neither Rob nor Kirsha moved.

'I'm afraid I can't allow that,' Rob said. 'It is my duty to protect you. As soon as I have a report that the area is clear we can go in. Until then I respectfully request that you remain in your ship.'

Ozer'o hissed with anger. 'Do I understand that you are attempting to stop me? From entering my own base? Beware of what you do, man.'

'I hope you won't consider it that way. There is great danger.'

Both the aliens had their hands pushed through slits in their heavy outer garments, their arms pulled tight against their bodies because of the cold. Rob could see them shudder. From the cold–or some other reason. It was an impasse. The men would not move. The Oinn were determined to pass. Then Ozer'o turned about as he spoke.

'Perhaps you are right, Colonel Hayward. We will remain inside out of the cold until you are ready.'

He said something in his own language to the Oinn next to him. While he was talking, Kirsha leaned over and took Rob by the arm.

Then threw his weight against him, knocking him to the ground. Shouting at the same time.

'Waste them! They're going to fire!'

Both Oinn had turned back, hands emerging with their laser weapons ready . . .

To jerk back, spin and fall as the bullets tore through their bodies, hammering them to the ground.

Sergeant Groot hurled himself from the truck, still firing into the aliens, kicking their weapons aside.

'I heard what he said to the other,' Kirsha shouted. 'He said to kill us, that they had been betrayed . . .'

A sudden flame lanced from the open doorway, burning into the Russian. Groot was returning the fire as the major fell, shooting into the open lock. Walking forward and spraying death from his sub machine-gun as he went.

'Take the ship!' Rob shouted. 'Forward!'

Destiny had taken any decision out of his hands. All he could do now was ride with it.

The Russian soldiers burst out of the door, roaring. Rob ran forward, tearing out his weapon, as Groot hurled himself through the door into the alien ship.

To be cut down by a sharp ray of fire. He arched, shuddered, fell.

The open portal began to swing down and close.

20. Prisoners

Sergeant Groot had fallen, half inside the hatchway and half out. Blood streamed from him, his clothing smoldered–but he wasn't dead. Not yet. As Rob ran towards him he saw the sergeant shiver as he tried to move, to draw his arm up. He tried again, and succeeded, lifting the gun up beside him.

Raising the muzzle of his sub machine-gun just as the door closed.

Down hard on the gun muzzle, jamming the butt against the sill. There was a mechanical whine of protest–and the door stopped moving. Held open by the gun. With the sergeant's dead hand still clasped tightly around it.

Rob was at the door, his .45 in his hand, firing at the retreating back of one of the Oinn inside the ship. The creature fell and there was the hammer of explosions by Rob's head as the first of the Russian soldiers leaned over him, firing quick bursts. Providing covering fire for a second soldier who was wriggling through the half-closed door.

The man made it through, was lifting his own gun– but to be cut down by a searing ray from inside the ship. Another soldier was already forcing his way in to take his place.

A corporal caught Rob by the shoulder and pulled him aside, holding him out of danger for the moment while the troopers led the assault. Rob clicked the release and jammed a new clip into the .45's butt as he called out.

'Kill them if they're armed,' he said. 'Kill them if they are at any controls. But get a prisoner–we need at least one prisoner!'

'I'll see to that, colonel,' the corporal said, releasing his grip and following the others into the ship. Rob pulled himself through the opening right after them.

Once the Oinn defenders at the entrance had been cut down the resistance collapsed. Few of the aliens deeper inside the ship were armed. They were killed anyway. The soldiers swept the vessel like a plague of death. Rob had to step over bodies on his way through the corridors. He found even more in the control room.

'I'll make my HQ here,' Rob said to the two soldiers on guard there. 'Get through the ship. Tell the noncoms. Move it.'

They raised their guns in a quick salute as they went out. Rob pushed a bleeding Oinn corpse onto the floor and dropped into the chair set before a control console. Now, with a moment to think, not react, he felt a cold jab of fear at what they had done. They had responded like soldiers, by conditioned reflex. Conditioned to defend themselves and kill the enemy.

But had they killed the Earth as well?

He looked up as a medic came through the door. He was half-supporting Major Danilov who was heavily bandaged from shoulder to waist.

'Kirsha! I thought you had bought it . . .'

Danilov lifted his hand wearily and dropped into an empty chair. 'To be frank, Rob, so did I. But the heavy clothes were some protection. Fried a lot of skin, but nothing too serious. Have we taken the ship?'

'We'll know soon. I sent out a runner.'

'Take these in one hour, major,' the medic said, shaking some white pills into Kirsha's hand. 'The shot I gave you will be wearing off then. There may be other casualties.' He turned, then ran out as another soldier appeared, calling to him from the doorway.

'What a stupid thing to have happen,' Krisha said. Rob nodded.

'Maybe the whole operation was doomed to work out this way. But we had to take the chance.'

The reports began to come in. The ship had been cleared. Casualties had been light. Very few of the aliens had been armed. Then a runner brought a message, snapping to attention and saluting as he did.

'We have some of them trapped and still alive, colonel. They sealed themselves in a compartment. They want to talk to the officer in charge.'

'Do they speak English?'

'Of a sort.'

'Take me there. Major, take command until I return.'

The sealed compartment was in the stern of the craft, the door high and massive. It could very well be the engine room. A dead Oinn was huddled against the wall and two soldiers came to attention when Rob appeared. One of them pointed to a panel beside the door.

'It's some kind of an intercom, colonel. They have been speaking to us through it.'

'Who is there now? Is that the officer?' The voice rasped from a barred grill. Rob stepped close to it.

'This is Colonel Hayward. I am the officer in charge.'

'I know you, colonel. Why you kill us? Such kind of awful death . . .'

'Your people fired on us. We returned the fire. We simply defended ourselves. Do you wish to surrender?'

'No more of killing!'

'If you are unarmed you will not be injured. You have my word on that.'

'There is a gun here.'

'Open the door and push it through. But remember, we will fire if there is any attempt to use it.'

'No. No shooting. We open the door.'

The soldiers had their guns raised and aimed as some interior mechanism hummed and the door opened a few inches. Then stopped. A trembling white hand appeared in the opening, holding a ray pistol by the barrel. It clattered down on the deck. Rob kicked it to one side.

'Show yourself,' he said. 'There will be no more killing.'

The Oinn slowly moved forward so he could be seen. His hands were raised, his mouth opening and closing rapidly. The flap on the side of his head fluttered as he spoke.

'See, I surrender,' he said. 'Others here also surrender. Six of us. We are workers of the engines only. Not soldiers of war. You will not kill us.'

'You have my word on that. Now open the door all the way.'

The Oinn was shaking–could it have been fear?–and its voice was trembling as well. 'No guns. But even if you anger at what you see you not kill us?'

What was the thing talking about? 'You have my word. No more shooting. Now open up.'

The Oinn called a command back over his shoulder, then stepped back from the door as it opened further. Rob flattened against the wall, his gun aimed. The two soldiers were prone on the floor ready to fire as well. The door opened all the way.

Rob looked in at the six aliens and understood why the Oinn had been so possessed with fear. He slowly let his gun drop, then pushed it back into its holster.

'Hold these prisoners here,' he ordered the soldiers. 'Don't harm them. Don't let them touch any apparatus. I'll send for them as soon as I can.'

He made his way back to the control room, going slowly while he decided what had to be done next. There were more soldiers there now, talking excitedly in the release of tension in the aftermath of battle. They quieted as he came in.

'Major Danilov,' Rob said, 'do you think you can take command here until I can send a relief?'

'Yes. No problem.'

'Good. I must report to General Beltine at once. I'll send you some more troops, medics, ambulances, and some transportation. I would stay, but my message takes first priority. We have our prisoners. Six of them who were holed up in the engine room. I have to get the report back.'

'Did they talk?'

Rob stopped in the doorway, smiling wryly.

'They didn't have to,' he said. 'Just one look was

enough. They were the engine room crew. Six of them, like I said.' Rob took a deep breath.

'Three of them were Oinn. But the other three were the Oinn's sworn enemies. Blettr. They weren't prisoners or anything like that. They were all working together. Side by side.'

21. The Ultimatum

'Colonel Hayward, I wish to protest most strongly the manner in which you have treated us.'

'Professor Tilleman, Doctor Lukoff, please come in. Would you like some coffee? This is a fresh pot.'

'Just abandon the small talk, colonel.' Tilleman was angry, his skin glowing with the heat of his internal fires, his gray hair standing out from his head. 'We are not treating this matter lightly.'

'Nor am I gentlemen. But I'm pouring some more coffee for myself. It was a little on the cold side out there.'

He started to pour a cup for Kirsha as well, until he saw that the Russian soldier's eyes were closed and he was leaning back on the couch that had been improvised for him. The four of them were alone in the large mess hall. It had insulated windows facing out on the dark antarctic night. Rob pointed towards these windows and the two scientists forgot their anger for the moment at the sight of the dark form of the Oinn space cruiser on the airfield beyond.

'All we have heard is rumors,' Lukoff said. 'Someone said that there had been fighting, the Oinn are here. You have been to their ship . . .'

'Let me tell you exactly what has happened since I saw you last.' Rob blew on the coffee, then sipped some. 'A silent alarm of some kind was actuated when we entered the Oinn area here. That ship out there responded to it, came here because of what they took to be an emergency. Of course they were right, but we couldn't tell them that. Major Danilov and I went out to talk to them. I am unhappy to report that our conversation was not very successful. They tried to kill us . . .'

'This is terrible!'

'It *was* terrible. We are very lucky that it turned out as well as it did. We are professional soldiers, which you will understand means that we are not easy to kill. There was some fighting which ended when we occupied their ship.'

Tilleman's anger was under icy control now. 'Are you telling me that you threatened the peace of the world–the entire future of mankind by engaging the Oinn in combat?'

Rob's answer was just as cold. 'I am. And it is just possible that we insured the future of mankind by winning the engagement. We have taken over the ship. We suffered some casualties, as did they.'

'You're insane!' Lukoff shouted. 'You are going to destroy us all! The Oinn will retaliate, their destructive bombs . . .'

'Have not been dropped yet. Since the ship landed we have had no other official contact with them. The end may be close, gentlemen, but it hasn't quite arrived yet. I have talked to the joint chiefs and their representatives are on the way here now. They ordered me to inform you of this, and to pass on the order that you are to examine the ship at once. This could be the opportunity we desperately need to understand their technology. We have men waiting aboard the cruiser to guide you to what appear to be supplies of spare parts. I suggest you take one each of everything there, in addition to investigating the operation of their technologies.'

'We don't need you to tell us how to do our work.' Tilleman spat the words. 'And why should we bother if the world is to end soon?'

'Not that soon,' Rob said quietly. 'I haven't told you yet what else we have already found aboard the ship. The crew, the engine room staff, were made up of both Oinn and Blettr. The Blettr, their sworn enemies, were not slaves or prisoners but simply working side by side with them.'

'I don't understand.' Dr. Lukoff was baffled. He

blinked through his heavy glasses, unable to comprehend this new information.

'Let me spell it out then. We have been hoaxed. We knew the two groups of aliens spoke the same language, but we did not understand why. I think we do now. They work together. Perhaps they share that fortress on the Moon. Which means that the entire invasion, everything that happened, it was all a gigantic hoax. As was their entire story about the war between their two races. The ship that landed in Central Park was a plant. The "defensive" setup here was a fake. The generators out there are just lumps of metal. So the "battle" in space was a fake. We have been conned— and conned very well.'

'But the cities,' Tilleman protested. 'Denver, Metz, Tomsk. They were destroyed. Millions killed. That was not a con. Why was it done?'

Rob was grim now, not even realizing that he had slammed the heavy coffee mug down on the table. 'You're right. That was no ruse, no con. It was cold-blooded murder. They did it to convince us of the seriousness of the war. And we were convinced, rightly enough. Which is why I feel no guilt or qualms of conscience about what we have done here. Enough of us have died. It does not bother me to see some of them go the same way.'

'But they will bomb more of our cities!' Lukoff protested.

'Why?' Rob asked, glaring at him. 'Why should they bother? I know that you are an intelligent man of science, and far brighter than a dim soldier like myself. So you should understand that they would accomplish nothing by bombing us now. We *know* about them, know that the different races are not engaged in a galactic war. We now know that they are allies. I am not saying that the threat of bombing may not occur again in the future. But we are safe for the moment. Safe until they talk to us. Which is why we need any information you can dig out of that ship. So if you will, please. Do your work. We will argue about its importance later. I'm sorry if you find that insulting, but I am just speaking plainly to underline the urgency. The next step is up to them. Please do what must be done before that time.'

Professor Tilleman started to protest, then thought better of it. 'You are right. We will not waste time in useless argument now. I will make my feelings known later about this insane, absolutely obscene business. Right now we go to work.' He turned on his heel and left.

When the door had slammed shut Kirsha opened one eye and sighed.

'You heard all that?' Rob asked.

'Indeed. But I felt too tired to be drawn into it. You were doing well enough without my help.'

'How do you feel?'

'Glorious! What a high. The doc stuck so many needles of drugs into me that I feel like a pincushion. Eventually skin grafts, he said. But for the moment the wet compresses are doing the job.'

'You should be in the hospital.'

'I will be. As soon as this is over. I'm sorry about your sergeant.'

Rob looked down into his coffee cup and nodded. 'Groot was a good man. He bought it–but he saved us all, maybe the entire damned world–on the way out. If we live through this I am going to do everything that I can to see that he gets the Congressional Medal of Honor.'

'And the Order of Lenin. He will be the first man, and probably the last, ever to receive the highest awards from both our countries.'

'Let's do it! It's the sort of thing he would have enjoyed. Particularly the Russian award. That will make a big hit back in his home town in South Africa!'

Bright beams of light burned through the darkness outside and they both turned to look as a supersonic jet dropped through the protective shield and roared the length of the field. Its afterburners kicked in and it screamed up and out into the darkness again.

'Taking a look at the runway,' Rob said. 'They'll have to come in downwind, from the other end, but there should be enough distance for them to land. At least there is no wind or storm on this side of the barrier.'

Short minutes later the landing lights appeared again and the jet sat down just inside the invisible curtain that kept the weather at bay. There wasn't that much room, but the pilot was good; the plane bucked to a halt a good hundred yards short of the obstacle on the runway.

'They'll be brought here,' Rob said. 'And I have a feeling that this entire mess is going to be resolved at last.'

General Beltine slammed through the door with General Sobolevski right behind him. Nadia Andrianova came last, closing the door quietly behind her.

'Any new developments here since we talked?' Beltine snapped.

'No, sir. No contact with the enemy. The scientific team is in the ship now as you ordered.'

'We have received a communication from them, through the Siberian station. We put an armed guard on Srparr, the alien there. He was agitated, even more so after he passed on a message to us from the Moon fortress. It's very brief. Nadia will read it.'

She lifted the piece of paper. 'Regret violence at antarctic station. Cease your operations there at once and your cities will be spared injury.' She looked up. 'The message is unsigned.'

Beltine nodded grimly. 'The kid gloves are off now. That is a raw threat. And even though it is unsigned the assumption is that we know they are both in this war on the same side.'

'Do we follow instructions?' Rob asked.

'Never!' The Russian general's nostrils flared with anger. 'The joint chiefs are in agreement on that. This is a bluff to force our hand. And it's not going to work. We have their ship and we are going to keep it until we get some satisfaction in return. I want every soldier we have to get out there, either inside or outside the spaceship. That thing is our ace in the hole.'

Rob grabbed up the phone and issued his orders. Half the troops into the ship. The other half to use the vehicles to set up a defensive line around the ship. The guard outside to be rotated every hour.

Nadia came over to him when he had hung the phone up again. Kirsha was briefing the two generals on the capture of the alien ship. Rob seized the chance to talk to her.

'We took some casualties,' he said. She nodded.

'I heard. Poor Groot . . .'

'He died exactly as he had lived. A professional soldier. You can't be sorry for him.'

'Why not?' Her face was suddenly livid with anger. 'I'm not a soldier. I don't kill people. I don't like killing. I don't even like to push people around–even the way you manhandled me on the Moon. If you men of war hadn't set up this murder operation, he and the others would still be alive.'

'And we would still be in the dark about this entire stupid war. Don't you realize that we have been supplying fissionable materials to the very people who bombed our cities, destroyed millions of our people? Think about that kind of killing, if it is killing that bothers you.'

'You didn't know that when you took the risks . . .'

'The discovery of the true facts justified the risks, don't you realize that? As the general says, it's a whole new ball game and we hold the ace out there . . .'

'Hayward!' General Beltine snapped out. 'They're here.'

They ran to the window. A ring of vehicles now surrounded the alien spacecraft, the defending soldiers unseen behind these defenses. Another alien spacecraft, a far smaller one, was drifting slowly overhead. It floated towards the grounded craft, then away again, moving alone the row of aircraft before the terminal. To settle slowly to the ground just beyond them.

'I'll get down there, general,' Rob said. 'I'll have a radioman with me. There'll be another radio up here.

I'll pass on your instructions to them. May I go?'

A junior officer cannot tell a general what to do–but he can suggest a course of action. Particularly when it follows military tradition not to send ranking officers to an opening parlay with the enemy. Beltine glanced at the Russian general, who nodded briefly.

'Do that,' Beltine ordered. 'Report when you get there. Let us know who comes out of the ship.'

Rob issued quick orders on the phone and the radio-equipped car was waiting outside the entrance when he got down there.

'Get over to that ship that just landed,' he said to the sergeant behind the wheel. 'Nice and slow. Stop when you are about ten yards away.' He picked up the phone and called in as they started forward.

'Colonel Hayward to radio operator. Can you hear me?'

'Yes, sir.'

'Is your external speaker on so the general officers can hear me as well?'

'It's on, colonel.'

'We're approaching the ship now. It is very much like the first one that landed in Central Park. Could be a sister ship. Proceeding to the front where the hatch is. Stopping here. The hatch is opening. One, no two figures coming out. I'm getting out of the car to meet them. I recognize one, the Blettr commander from the Moon. Uplynn. The other one is an Oinn . . .'

'You, man!' the Blettr called out, marching over to Rob, standing above him and glaring down. 'Tell those you talk to that there is only one hour to do as I order. Obey me or Moscow and Washington D.C. will be destroyed. Tell them this thing.

'Tell them that we rule this planet Earth now and you will follow our instructions.'

22. No Reprieve

'I will pass on your message,' Rob told them, then repeated Uplynn's words into the radio handset. He listened to the response before he spoke again.

'I am not authorized to negotiate with you. I have been instructed to ask you to accompany me to the base where General Beltine and General Sobolevski will discuss your terms . . .'

'They come here!'

Rob's face was expressionless as he transmitted the messages between the two groups. 'General Beltine asks me to inform you that it is far more comfortable inside the building. You have his word, and that of General Danilov, that you will not be harmed.'

The two aliens conferred together briefly–then agreed. Rob controlled his elation as he reported the fact, then hung up the phone and walked with them back to the entrance. They had made no attempt to force their firm opening demands, but had capitulated at once. It could be a sign of how the discussions were to go. He led the way to the mess hall where the others were waiting. General Danilov took the offensive at once.

'You will now tell the truth. You will tell us the real reasons why you came to Earth, the reasons why you have lied to us ever since you came, the reasons why you destroyed three of our cities. Speak.'

Uplynn brushed the general's words aside with a wave of his great hand.

'Silence, creature of Earth. It is I who issue orders at this moment . . .'

'No,' General Beltine said, his voice cold as death. He stamped forward to stand before the tall alien, looking up into his face. 'The time for your lying is over. We have done as you have asked in the past only in order to gain time. We are now ready. I am informing you now that we have transported to the Moon two hundred high yield atomic bombs. Hydrogen bombs. They are now located in a circle around your Moon fortress, at an average distance of one kilometre from the fortress. When they are detonated it will cease to exist. Do you understand what I am saying?'

His words exacted a dramatic response from the envoys. The tall Blettr swayed as though he had been struck. The pallid Oinn jerked its head about–then ran for the door. Rob crashed his fist into the side of its neck as it passed, knocking the creature to the floor. He then pointed to the armed guards, weapons aimed, who had stepped into view outside the door.

'We lied to you,' General Beltine said. 'You are not safe here. Your lives are in jeopardy. If either of you speaks a single lie he will be killed. The time for telling the truth is now.'

General Danilov stamped forward and signaled Rob to drag the shivering Oinn to its feet. He shouted at it, his face just inches distant.

'The Oinn and the Blettr are in league against us. They do not war with each other. The ship that crashed was a plant to make us believe in the war. The war that was fought from here against the fortress on the moon was a fake. The weapons here are fakes. You did all of this to extract raw materials from us, to trick us into supplying you with fissionable material. Now answer. Is this the truth?'

The Oinn started to speak–but the Blettr commander shouted an order. The Oinn wouldn't listen. He called back in the same language. There was a brief exchange, then they both fell silent. Nadia stepped forward.

'Uplynn the Blettr ordered this Oinn, named Oged'u, to be silent and admit nothing. Oged'u responded that we know already, that all is lost, it is the end . . .'

Screeching shrilly, Uplynn hurled himself forward, claw-tipped fingers hooked to seize and kill.

The pistol shots cracked out, one after another, and

142

the bullets thudded into the tall alien, spun him about and brought him bleeding and dead to the floor. So close was he when he fell that drops of green blood spattered the cringing Oinn. Kirsha Danilov dropped back into his supporting cushions, breathing heavily, the automatic limp in his hand. He pointed it at the corpse when he spoke.

'Uplynn called that one a traitor and a weakling as he attacked. Said that he would kill him so he could not speak. I thought it better that the Blettr die instead.'

'You were perfectly right,' General Beltine said, crossing the floor and reaching down to the cringing Oinn. 'I shall not hurt you,' he said. 'I am only helping you to stand. To sit here comfortably. Good. Now . . . speak.'

He pulled a chair up close before the Oinn, as did General Sobolevski. The room was silent, hushed. Beltine spoke softly, intimately.

'The Oinn and Blettr are not at war. They live in peace, is that not so?'

'Yes.'

'Good. You pretended to be at war in order to get fissionable materials from us. True?'

'There was a war, a long time ago. It was terrible. A few survived. All of the records are lost. We no longer know who was fighting against whom. We do not know if our home planets still survive. We do not even know where they are . . .'

'You're soldiers, retreating–or probably deserting!' Rob hardly knew that he had spoken aloud. 'You have just that one fortress, a few ships, little fuel . . .'

Rob fell silent, knowing he should not have spoken. But the realization of the truth had driven all of the years of training and discipline from him. In the silence that followed his outburst, Oged'u's voice was thin and clear.

'A handful, less each generation. The radiation, something. They say it has deformed genes, many of us born incomplete, we must have metal limbs made. But the machines don't always work. Some we cannot repair. Only four ships left. Three now. One almost impossible to repair. We used it to bait the trap. We had to survive. Release me. We will leave. We have the fuel. Let us go. We should not have come here. Your race is too fierce, you like to kill. Release me.'

'That is not for us to decide,' Sobolevski said. 'We simply speak for our governments. Until they instruct us you will be kept here. Be glad at least that you are still alive.'

He nudged the Blettr corpse with his toe as a grim reminder.

It took twenty-hours to reach a decision. This was a miracle of speed considering the fact that a special, all night meeting of the United Nations was convened. While the delegates were debating, a supersonic jet arrived at the antarctic station from Siberia bearing Srparr, the Blettr representative on Earth, along with his communication device. He conferred with Oged'u, who gave him a censored version of what had occurred at the station. Nadia eavesdropped shamelessly while they talked, then made her report to the generals in the adjoining room.

'The Oinn are adroit liars. Oged'u now claims that we discovered everything on our own, that he told us nothing, that Uplynn attacked us in anger and we had to defend ourselves. Srparr is now reporting the incident to the fortress.'

'Very good,' General Beltine said. 'Oged'u will side with us in the negotiations in order to protect himself.'

'He will,' Nadia agreed. 'He will also lie to us with equal facility.'

'We know that. Precautions have been taken.' He did not volunteer as to what they were and she did not ask.

When the decision of the United Nations was agreed upon, the meeting was assembled again. General Sobolevski read this decision aloud in slow and careful English while Nadia made notes.

'I have been instructed to inform you that the following agreement has been reached this day. We, the peoples of Earth, do not wish to indulge in any continuing

144

warfare with the forces of the Blettr and Oinn. Therefore the hydrogen bombs on the Moon will not be detonated if the fortress there leaves the Moon and this solar system at once. The prisoners at the antarctic station will be permitted to board the cruiser and leave. The smaller spacecraft will remain where it is as small repayment for the losses the Earth has suffered.'
Sobolevski carefully laid the sheet of paper down. 'That is the end of the communication. You will now transmit it to your authorities. Tovarich Andrianova has prepared a translation which you will use.'

Nadia passed the translation to Srparr who switched on his communicator. Rob stopped him as he reached for his headphones.

'Our technicians have established that this apparatus is equipped with a loudspeaker. That will be used, not these earphones. We wish to hear both sides of the conversation.'

Srparr gave him a look of what could only have been cold malice, before throwing other switches on the communicator. There was silence as he read out the message.

There were protests from the Moon, but they were beaten down. The United Nations had been firm; no compromises or emendations would be permitted. In the end they could only agree.

'You leave us little choice,' Oged'u said.

'This war was your choice–the ending of it is ours,' was General Beltine's unsympathetic response. He turned to Rob. 'Have Professor Tilleman's operational teams reported in, Colonel Hayward?'

'They have, sir. All teams have withdrawn. All work is complete.'

'Good. You will accompany Oged'u to the vessel and see to the release of the captives there. Then you will withdraw all troops from the vessel. Report when this has been done.'

'But I am here!' Srparr protested.

'You will remain here,' the General said, 'until the fortress has left the Moon. We wish to keep the communication link with your people open. After they have gone your ship will pick you up. Not before.'

The Blettr had no choice. He could only watch through the window as Oged'u was taken to the cruiser as the troops there were leaving. When Rob returned he reported that the operation was complete.

'All of our units withdrawn from the enemy craft, general.'

'All right.' Beltine turned to the Blettr. 'Signal your ship that it may leave now.'

They could see the open hatchway swing shut. Within a minute the cruiser stirred and lifted into the air, then vanished upward through the shield. Srparr stayed at the communicator. Its speaker rustled with sound very soon after this, passing a message in his language.

'They are clear of the atmosphere,' Nadia translated. 'In orbit around Earth.'

'No,' General Sobolevski said. 'They are to proceed to the Moon, that is the agreement.'

Before the command could be sent, Oged'u's voice spoke from the transmitter. In English. Firmly. All traces of the cringing whine had vanished.

'This craft is now in low Earth orbit. You will transmit a message to your United Nations that I was forced to be less than truthful because of the necessity of our survival. We have more of the city-destroying bombs than I told you. But all of them were aboard this ship so you can see we negotiated under a severe handicap. That handicap has now been removed. We issue the orders now.'

As he paused for a moment there was absolute silence in the room. When he continued his voice rang with sadistic glee.

'You will issue orders that all of the hydrogen bombs will be removed from the Moon. When this has been accomplished we will issue further orders. You will do this, because if you don't every one of your major cities will be bombed, the millions of inhabitants killed. They will be emptied of life within the hour.'

23.   Final Glory

In the dead silence that followed this announcement, General Beltine stood up and slowly crossed the room towards the communicator. Srparr stepped back before his steady advance.

'You will not hurt me. Nothing you do to me will change anything. You heard Oged'u. Our ship has the bombs. Do as he says or millions of millions will die here on Earth.'

Beltine ignored him, waving him aside as he picked up the microphone.

'It does not come as a surprise to us that you were lying yet again,' the general said. 'We took that fact into consideration when we drew up our plans. We concealed certain important facts, waiting until we had determined what your true aims were. Now, we know. Now we are certain once and for all, though little doubt existed before, that you cannot be trusted in any way at any time. We cannot negotiate with you. We can only use force and order you what to do. We have certain weapons that we have concealed from you for reasons that are obvious now. One of them is an energy weapon that can destroy any ship in space. I am now ordering Colonel Hayward to fire this weapon at your cruiser. Colonel, take that ship out.'

Rob had been speaking quietly on the telephone while they had been listening to the general. Now all eyes were on him as he spoke a single, sharp command.

'Fire.'

Oged'u's angry voice rasped from the speaker.

'Your stupid bluff will not work . . .'

It cut off. Srparr was the first to stir, groping to the transmitter, speaking into it, shouting, then shifting channels. A different voice answered him, high-pitched and wailing.

'That was the Moon fortress,' Nadia said. 'Reporting that the cruiser has been destroyed. Their other ship saw it happen.'

Srparr was shouting now, screaming into the microphone. There was a babble of voices over the speaker, but none of them seemed to be addressing him.

'They are in a panic as you can hear,' Nadia said. 'They are not making sense.'

The transmission cut off suddenly, and in the silence the telephone bell sounded shockingly loud. Rob picked it up and listened, then handed it to General Sobolevski. He listened to the brief message, nodded and hung up.

'That was our lunar observation station. The fortress has left, without any warning. At full power. They are gone ...' The ringing phone cut him off. Rob answered it again.

'Mount Palomar Observatory,' he said. 'The fortress sighted on an ecliptic course, leaving the solar system. Its acceleration is continuing. Undoubtedly full power as the lunar base reported.'

It was then that they cheered. Shaking hands, pounding each other on the back. It was victory, victory against extermination, victory against the immense power of this terrible enemy. Final victory!

Only Nadia did not join in the cheering. Too many were dead for her to find anything to celebrate. And she was looking at Srparr the Blettr. The giant creature had dropped into the chair, was slumped forward, unmoving. She could barely hear the single word he spoke–but she knew the meaning.

Alone. Alone as no other creature had ever been. Trapped on an alien world by an alien race, while the others of its kind vanished out among the stars. She understood how he felt. But she could not sympathize in the slightest. Just as she could not celebrate with the others. The legions of the dead stood in the way. She looked up and found Rob's eyes upon her. He called out to the armed soldiers at the door.

'Take the prisoner away and lock him up. Under heavy guard. We don't want any suicides, understand? We want him available and alive for our scientists. He will be useful to us.'

Nadia waited in silence until the last enemy had gone. Only then did she ask Rob what she needed to know.

'What is this weapon that blew up the cruiser? I knew nothing about it.' He smiled, an unhumorous smile.

'Neither did I–up until a few hours ago. We couldn't trust these creatures. We wired an atomic bomb inside the engine room of the cruiser, connected to one of their aerials on the hull. After that it was up to them. We suspected treachery. We were right. So we sent out a coded radio signal and blew the ship up. With this evidence of our military superiority the rest of them panicked. They're gone now. The threat is over.'

Her eyes widened in sudden realization. 'You people have been lying to them right along. Beating them at their own game.'

Rob nodded. 'What other weapon did we have that could touch them? They had all the cards, all the bombs. We had to fight back in any way that we could.'

'What about the hydrogen bombs on the Moon? Were they really there–or was that just a bluff as well?'

General Beltine had been listening, and he broke in. 'I am afraid, my dear, that is a military secret that will have to remain secret. You have been of immense help to us and we cannot thank you enough. The threat is removed, the war is over, we have scientific evaluations of their technology as well as their ship to examine. If they–or any other alien race–should try to invade us again they will find us ready and waiting.'

'To kill–and keep on killing?' She drew back, horrified. The general nodded grimly.

'If we must. It is our job to defend.'

'Defend means to kill. You and your men–' she looked

149

at Rob, '– know how to kill. But tell me. How many people have you ever brought to life?'

General Beltine snorted and turned away. He had no time to waste bandying words with pacifists. It was Rob who spoke.

'We had no choice. You understand that?'

'Do I? I don't really think that I do. They came in fear, and killed in fear in order to establish control. But the dead millions can never be restored to life. Nor can the people killed here when the decision was made to attack. That made still more dead. Something else might have been done. The aliens were few in number. They feared us. They might have been taught not to. We might have educated them to live alongside us. They could have taught us their science–and we might have taught them some of our humanity.'

'But we didn't. That's history now. The past is past and it can't be changed.'

'Yes, of course,' she said, turning from him towards the door. She started to walk away, then stopped and looked back for an instant.

'But don't you have any qualms? Doubts? Don't you realize just how wonderful it would have been if we had taken this opportunity, just once in mankind's bloody history, to succeed by peace and not by war?

'To hold out the hand of brotherhood to the galaxy. Not the streaming red hand of death.'

Then Nadia turned and left and Colonel Hayward stood and watched her go. He did not go after her. He had no doubts. He had been there. He knew exactly what had happened.

Yes, of course, it *was* victory.

Wasn't it?

BOOK 1:

Cloud Warrior

PATRICK TILLEY

Ten centuries ago the Old Time ended
when Earth's cities melted in the War of
a Thousand Suns. Now the lethal high
technology of the Amtrak Federation's
underground stronghold is unleashed
on Earth's other survivors – the surface-
dwelling Mutes. But the primitive
Mutes possess ancient powers far
greater than any machine . . .

FICTION   0 7221 8516 2   £1.95

PLANET OF NO RETURN

NO RETURN

Harry Harrison

Landing on a new planet is a danger every time,
and Selm-II is no exception.

The specialist didn't like it. There were no cities
visible from space, no broadcasts or transmissions
on the blank airwaves – yet the wrecked war
machines of an advanced technology littered the
rich pastures of the deserted planet. Hundreds,
perhaps thousands, of crumpled and gigantic
weapons of war, a graveyard of destruction
stretching almost to the lifeless horizon. But the
war wasn't over . . . and they weren't all wrecks!
It's an emergency. It's a job for Brion Brand, the
mightiest weightlifter in the galaxy. With the
brilliant, sensuous Dr Lea Morees at his side he
plunges into the war zone, into the steel jaws of
the PLANET OF NO RETURN!

SCIENCE FICTION   0 7221 4537 3   £1.50

Vaneglory

GEORGE TURNER

A SEARING FUTURISTIC VISION
OF THE POST-ATOMIC WORLD

The year is 2037. The place – Australia: one of the few land masses uncontaminated by the silent palls of lethal radioactive dust which spread swift death across most of the habitable world back in the 1980s.

It's a bleak and alien society for Will and Donald, awoken from a 45-year sleep with searing memories of nuclear death and destruction forever burned deep into their scarred minds. Faced with a psycho-controlled authoritarian society where none are more hated than the 'barbaric' survivors of Armageddon, scapegoats for every birth-pang of the new era, their chances of survival in the brave new world are slim . . .

VANEGLORY – a brilliant fantasy about the nightmare reality of a dream of power come true.

SCIENCE FICTION   0 7221 8643 6   £2.25

A selection of bestsellers from SPHERE

FICTION

SOLITAIRE	Graham Masterton	£1.95 ☐
THE QUEEN'S MESSENGER	Robert L. Duncan	£1.95 ☐
THE LAST GASP	Trevor Hoyle	£2.50 ☐
CROSSINGS	Danielle Steel	£1.95 ☐
THE SIRENS OF AUTUMN	Tom Barling	£1.95 ☐

FILM AND TV TIE-INS

MINDER	Anthony Masters	£1.50 ☐
THE KILLING OF KAREN SILKWOOD	Richard Rashke	£1.95 ☐
SCARFACE	Paul Monette	£1.75 ☐
BY THE SWORD DIVIDED	Mollie Hardwick	£1.75 ☐
AUF WIEDERSEHEN, PET	Fred Taylor	£1.75 ☐

NON-FICTION

TWINS	Peter Watson	£1.75 ☐
SHADOWS ON THE GRASS	Simon Raven	£1.95 ☐
THE GOEBBELS DIARIES	Fred Taylor (Ed)	£3.95 ☐
THE BOOK OF ROYAL LISTS	Craig Brown & Lesley Cunliffe	£2.50 ☐
HOW TO MAKE A SECOND INCOME	Godfrey Golzen	£1.95 ☐

All Sphere books are available at your local bookshop or newsagent, or can be ordered direct from the publisher. Just tick the titles you want and fill in the form below.

Name _____

Address _____

_____

Write to Sphere Books, Cash Sales Department, P.O. Box 11, Falmouth, Cornwall TR10 9EN

Please enclose a cheque or postal order to the value of the cover price plus:

UK: 45p for the first book, 20p for the second book and 14p for each additional book ordered to a maximum charge of £1.63.

OVERSEAS: 75p for the first book plus 21p per copy for each additional book.

BFPO & EIRE: 45p for the first book, 20p for the second book plus 14p per copy for the next 7 books, thereafter 8p per book.

Sphere Books reserve the right to show new retail prices on covers which may differ from those previously advertised in the text or elsewhere, and to increase postal rates in accordance with the PO.